Praise for
Stella Peabody's Wild Librarian Bakery and Bookstore

"Flamboyant ex-librarian fosters community in this novel of linked stories....It's a gathering place for monthly feminist book clubs, vision board classes, art openings, and, most importantly, cafe regulars who evolve over the years....At the end of the book prolific author Russo writes about her own desire to start a business like the Wild Librarian—a safe space for creativity and community, resplendent with plenty of words, vegan goodies, and most of all, people....Russo's exuberance shines through the antics of the quirky, diverse cast and especially Stella herself....Ideal for those who love combining feminism, reading, and sweet treats."

Kirkus Reviews

"A sense of whimsy blends nicely with the ingredients of solid characterization and good reads, much in the manner of a cozy mystery, but without the intrigue portion powering the tale. 'Cozy' is brought to life in the descriptions, evolutionary processes, and book-and-food-based world of characters who each revolve around books and/or food in different ways. From new recipes 'inspired by adventure' to travels that result in new shared stories that spark imagination and change, a bookstore's commitment to community, baking, and love translates to vignettes about individuals who are changed not just by the store's presence, but by its varied offerings.

Book and food enthusiasts alike will find much to relish in *Stella Peabody's Wild Librarian Bakery and Bookstore: A Novel-in-Stories.* As its characters and world evolves, so does a sense of *joie de vivre* that inspires art in various forms, pays tribute to women's lives, and centers on the powers of imagination, questions, and cultivating creative fun in peoples' lives. *Stella Peabody's Wild Librarian Bakery and Bookstore*'s delight resides in its delicious sense of community and depiction of women's connections. It will reach its appealing aroma into the minds and hearts of readers that enjoy good books, tasty recipes, and compelling stories alike."

D. Donovan, Senior Reviewer, *Midwest Book Review*

"A close observation of modern life, laced with compassion, forgiveness, and belonging. A story of creating community through art and imagination."

Mary Camarillo, author of *The Lockhart Women*

"I just entered Stella Peabody's world and feel so at home. I can anticipate there never being enough pages to keep me there in that wonderful place! In *Stella Peabody's Wild Librarian Bakery and Bookstore*. Stacy Russo has given us what an individual needs most in this world: community - safe, beautiful, and delicious!"

Ruth King, Blues Musician and Recording Artist

"Russo transports her readers to a deliciously interconnected web of people and place where vulnerable human experience is celebrated alongside decadent desserts. *Stella Peabody's Wild Librarian Bakery and Bookstore* is a wonderful and deeply relatable read."

Charissa Lucille, *Wasted Ink Zine Distro*

"There's something cozy and safe yet also wise, realistic, and visionary about Stacy Russo's novel-in-stories, *Stella Peabody's Wild Librarian Bakery and Bookstore*. Clearly written with precision and clarity, the stories provide a model for how to live and interact, an ideal after which to model ourselves, and ways to get through our suffering. The characters are vivid and memorable. The vegan recipes for food (and for life) are a reassuring delight."

Lucretia Tye Jasmine, Freelance Writer and Artist, and Co-producer of KPFK's *Feminist Magazine*

"A much needed new fiction: enchanting, experimental, and sensitive. The 'wild librarian,' the bookstore/bakery, and a warm community — intricately woven in the seven stories — are as welcoming as hearth, as essential as books and baking, as necessary and generous as the sharing of recipes and nourishment: Both material and spiritual. The place, Santa Ana, is vividly (re)imagined and indisputably real. The novel is magical and balm for our shattered world in need of healing."

Jie Tian, Poet, Librarian, Bookmaker

"Each story depicts various scenarios: a missing wife and her heartbroken husband; an adventurous trip with the women's book club to Taos, New Mexico; and an artist's life journey ... Author Stacy Russo has crafted a compelling novel in *Stella Peabody's Wild Librarian Bakery and Bookstore*. This is a book to be savored in the same way her customers enjoy her bakery items!"

Deborah Lloyd for *Readers' Favorite — 5 Starred Review*

Also by Stacy Russo

NONFICTION

A Better World Starts Here: Activists and Their Work
(Sanctuary Publishers)

Love Activism (Litwin Books)

We Were Going to Change the World: Interviews with Women from the 1970s and 1980s Southern California Punk Rock Scene
(Santa Monica Press)

The Library as Place in California (McFarland & Company)

EDITED COLLECTIONS

Feminist Pilgrimage: Journeys of Discovery (Litwin Books)

Life as Activism: June Jordan's Writings from The Progressive
(Litwin Books)

POETRY

The Moon and Other Poems (Dancing Girl Press)

Everyday Magic (Finishing Line Press)

CHILDREN'S BOOKS

Wild Librarian Bakery and Bookstore (Litwin Books)

Poetry Hounds (Litwin Books)

Stella Peabody's Wild Librarian Bakery and Bookstore

A Novel-in-Stories

Cover and interior page design by Nancy Smith.

Cover art by Tori Holder (www.toriholder.com).

Editorial services by Bryony Leah (www.bryonyleah.com).

Published by Wild Librarian Press, Santa Ana, California.

www.wildlibrarianpress.com

Wild Librarian Press
Santa Ana, California

Thank you for supporting a woman-owned independent press!

Publisher's Cataloging-in-Publication data

Names: Russo, Stacy Shotsberger, 1970-, author.

Title: Stella Peabody's Wild Librarian Bakery and Bookstore : A Novel-in-Stories / by Stacy Russo.

Description: Santa Ana, CA: Wild Librarian Press, 2021.

Identifiers: LCCN: 2021915371 | ISBN: 978-1-7376759-0-7 (paperback) | 978-1-7376759-1-4 (ebook)

Subjects: Bookstores--Fiction. | Bakeries--Fiction. | Librarians--Fiction. | Women--Fiction. | BISAC FICTION / General | FICTION / Women

Classification: LCC PS3618.U77445 S74 2021 | DDC 813.6--dc23

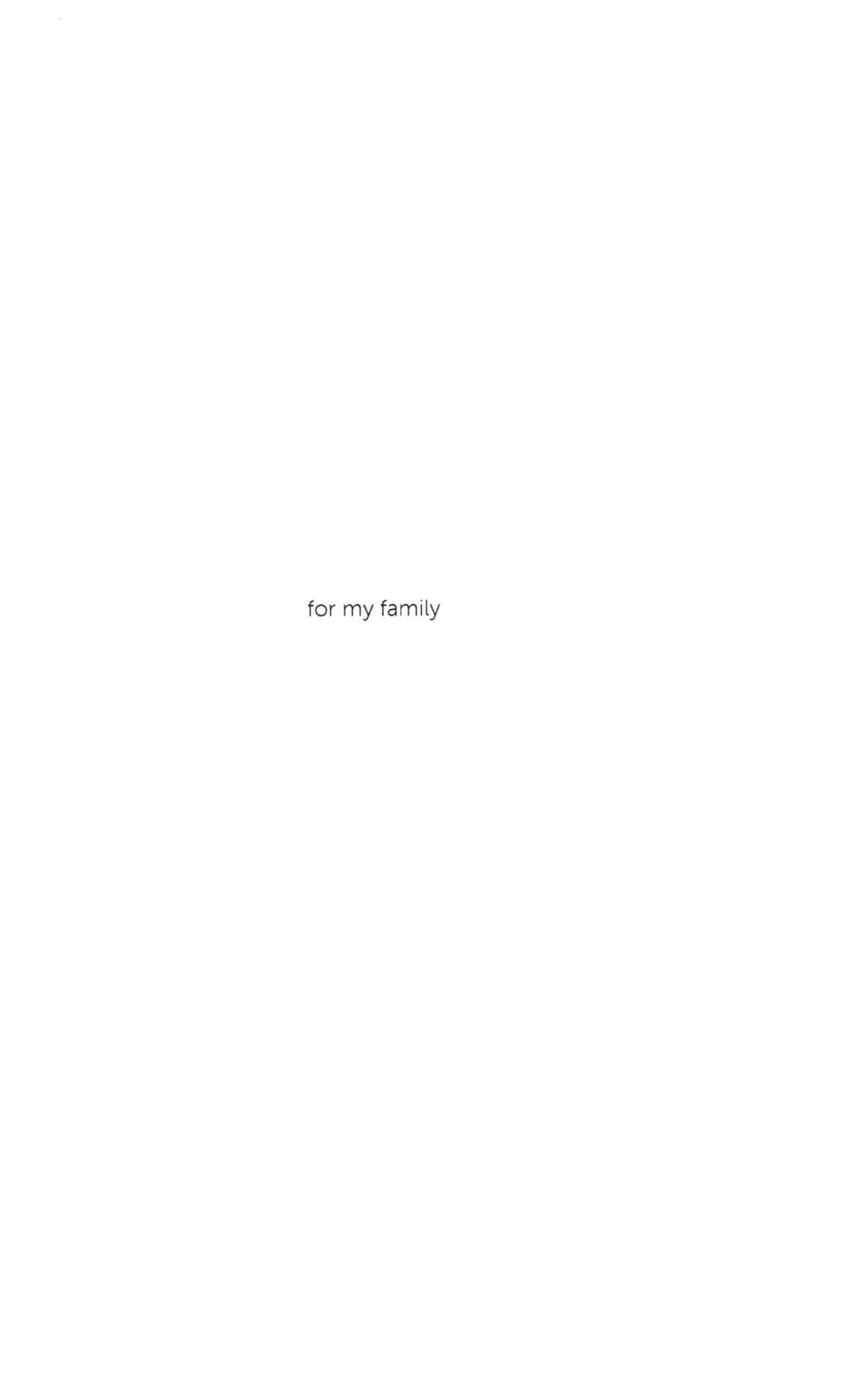

for my family

CONTENTS

"The wild woman is fluent in the language of dreams, images, passion, and poetry."

Clarissa Pinkola Estés

"Chocolate before noon."

Stella Peabody

Not too far from the City of Angels, on a purple tree-lined street in the heart of Santa Ana, California, you can find Stella Peabody's magical Wild Librarian Bakery and Bookstore in between Riviera's Spice Shop and Luna's Italian Restaurant.

The Closet Romantic

Stella Peabody stood near the tall bookshelves holding a round silver tray of assorted muffins and cupcakes. She was wearing her usual faded blue jeans, a T-shirt, tan construction boots, a pair of long, jangly earrings, and one of the promotional buttons for the bakery that declared her personal motto: "Chocolate before noon!" Four blue balloons, selected to match the exterior of the Wild Librarian Bakery and Bookstore, and one purple heart-shaped balloon, to match the color of the front door, bobbed in the air from a string around her wrist. She thought the balloons were a bit silly, but Grace Nguyen, a bakery employee known as Stella's right-hand woman, thought it would be a fun touch. The reporter and photographer agreed.

It was the second anniversary of the Wild Librarian's opening, and Stella was being interviewed for the *Los Angeles Times* food section. Her brother Ben flew down from Seattle the night before. He watched everything unfold from one of the tables, proud of his older sister. The young photographer was wearing a yellow sundress that brushed against the floor as she moved to capture Stella at different angles. Stella couldn't help but notice how the dress matched the Enchanted Lemon Pecan Cupcakes, named after Thomas Moore's book *The Re-enchantment of Everyday Life*, that were lined up on one side of her silver tray.

A former librarian, Stella named most of her baked goods after her favorite books and writers. For today's celebration, she'd also prepared fresh batches of Coconut Jazz Muffins inspired by the writer Toni Morrison, Magical Day Muffins named in honor of Mary Oliver's poetry, and On the Road Chocolate Cupcakes inspired by Jack Kerouac's novel of the Beat Generation. Her favorite album, Joni Mitchell's *Blue,* played softly over the bakery's stereo system.

The photographer motioned for Stella to pose for more photographs outside the entrance. The light marine layer from the ocean kept the sun soft and partially hidden. "Perfect lighting," Stella heard the reporter say. Grace joined her outside along with Andy Anderson and his partner, Alex, a young couple in their late twenties who were known by everyone as the Two A's. Like Grace, Andy, the assistant baker and event coordinator, had been with Stella since the beginning of the Wild Librarian. Alex, an artist and master carpenter, had made the exquisite bookshelves and much of the handsome wood furniture for the interior.

Several of Stella's loyal customers and members of the bakery community had been invited to the festivities. They started trailing in. The McDaniels, an elderly couple who lived in the nearby senior apartments, were the first to arrive. Eleanor McDaniels' wooden walking stick made its usual loud, rhythmic vibrations as the couple made their way to the bakery's few coveted overstuffed reading chairs. Elly Kim and Mary Chin from Stella's book club sat at a table near the bookshelves, sipping coffee. A local artist, Clare Fortune, who taught workshops at the bakery, glided in wearing one of her signature linen tunics. Stella was surprised to see Guy Mandal, a shy and self-described "traveling musician" who played music for passersby from various benches at a local park, had accepted her invite to the celebration. He walked in with the accordion he always carried. And Robert Gonzales and his wife Maria, who had recently celebrated their thirtieth wedding anniversary, were gathered with some of Stella's former librarian colleagues at the bakery's large community table.

"It looks like the only VIP missing is Jane," Andy announced. The joke was lost on the reporter and photographer, but everyone else laughed. Jane was Stella's large, white, and fluffy German shepherd dog.

Before leaving, the reporter asked everyone to behave naturally so the photographer could get a shot. "Please don't pose," he called out as the photographer clicked away, "Natural. Natural." It felt like show business to Eleanor. She giggled and picked up her fork, attempting to nibble at her muffin in a casual way. Grace pretended to ring Clare up at the register. Mary and Elly balanced books in one hand and coffee mugs in the other. Guy turned sideways from the camera and pulled his accordion onto his lap. Stella's brother looked down at his phone. When the article appeared later that week, everyone in the photograph was engaged in some activity, except for Robert and Maria who looked directly at the camera with his arms wrapped tightly around her.

Stella knew Robert Gonzales from the community college where they were former colleagues. When Stella left to follow her dream and open the Wild Librarian, he became a frequent and loyal customer. Robert liked to leave large bills in the tip jar and give generously for the bakery's "pay what you can" coffee. Stella showed her appreciation but kindly told him it was not necessary. "It gives me great pleasure," was his explanation, and the excessive tips continued. When Robert stopped by, often in the mornings, his usual was two servings of Poet's Beer Bread and a large black coffee. He liked to get a table by the window and watch the city come to life.

During the holidays, Stella spiced up the beer bread, adding cherries and cranberries. Robert took one bite the first time he had the holiday bread, closed his eyes, and filled the bakery with his voice: "Heaven!"

Robert had taught welding at the college for over twenty years. His favorite class to teach was Beginning Pipe Fundamentals since he loved the students who were just starting out, especially the older reentry students. These returning students, some with defined wrinkles already setting in, reminded Robert of himself when he left his job at a local construction company to try his hand at teaching. Their older faces, even when tired, reflected second chances and dreams.

Robert was close to retirement when Stella resigned from her position at the library to open the bakery. When he came into the Wild Librarian one day with an invitation to his retirement party on campus, she rang the bell next to the cash register several times and let out a cheer.

The evening before his campus retirement party, a smaller group of Robert's most beloved students and colleagues from the welding department gathered at the bakery. As people began to arrive, the classical guitarist Stella had hired as a surprise was already set up near the bookshelves to greet everyone with a soft serenade. Stella brought out a large tray of freshly baked Poet's Beer Bread, still warm in the center, and placed it on the table in front of where Robert sat with Maria. Everyone enjoyed large plates of pasta with marinara sauce, catered by Luna's Italian Restaurant next door. As the celebration moved beyond pasta to dive into the generously frosted chocolate cake Stella made earlier in the day, Guy Mandal arrived with his accordion to replace the guitarist. A few people who were not part of the celebration wandered in with curiosity, as if pulled through the doors by the warm electricity of the gathering. Stella offered them chairs, and they joined in until the party ended close to midnight, with many people on their feet dancing along with Guy's accordion tunes. He added a rhythmic beat by tapping his heavy boots on the floor as he played his beloved instrument.

Robert's formal retirement party on campus the following afternoon was held outside in the main quad area. There were balloons, the faculty jazz band played, and the chancellor and president spoke. Stella attended and overheard someone in the crowd whisper in a puzzled tone, "Look at all this. Why do you think he's loved so much?" She didn't turn around, but she was almost certain it was the voice of the ceramics professor, Malcolm Boyd, because of the thick Scottish accent. She found his question rude and out of place considering the joyous occasion and admiration for Robert. She wondered who he might be talking to or if he was speaking out loud to himself.

Robert was the kind of man who wore his shoes until they couldn't be repaired. He took his lunch to work in an old-school metal flip-lid box as if he were going to a construction site. He kept a small black plastic comb in his pocket. It was common to see him walking across campus dragging the comb through his thinning hair.

He appeared to be a regular Joe, but there was a secret ingredient only his wife knew that may have been what made people easily warm up to him: Robert was a closet romantic. His romantic inklings only expanded as he aged, until much of his time away from the classroom and lab was focused on love. This was love of the pop culture variety. He was an avid viewer of made-for-TV movies on the Lifetime and Hallmark channels, especially if the movie had a marriage plot. He read romance novels in bed. Every Friday night since they were newlyweds, he'd brought Maria a bouquet of flowers to mark the beginning of their weekend. Above all else in his life, showering Maria with love was the central rhythm of his thoughts and actions. "My daily poetry," he once told Stella.

Even though he fully engaged in his romantic inclinations with Maria, Robert also believed something may be off about it, so he kept this part of his life hidden from public view. While growing up, his father made sure to hide what he described as "soft feelings." Robert's adult life was surrounded by similar ideas of masculinity. Once, while driving a fellow worker home from a construction site, the guy spotted a romance novel on the floor of Robert's truck and chuckled. "My girl reads this shit too," he said. Robert laughed back and did not share that the copy of *Moonlight Magic* was his. He rather liked the stereotypical cover image of a man embracing a woman with a crescent moon in the sky above them. He couldn't wait to pick up where he left off when he got home.

There were days in Beginning Pipe Fundamentals when Robert was more animated than usual. He felt his toes buzzing in his shoes as he danced around the room. His students would leave the classroom with a charge, as if they were ignited by his spirit. They may have assumed it was simply his enthusiasm for teaching and the work they were doing, but that was only partly true. No one would have guessed Robert's day was filled with electricity because he knew *When a Man Loves a Woman* was on Lifetime at 8:00 p.m. that night.

Stella and Robert got to know each other when they were tasked to lead a campus faculty committee. Stella was known as a renegade on campus; she was often seen in her jeans and construction boots marching with students in protests. She led student clubs in feminism and animal rights. She taught a class on banned books through the English department, and another on radical women's memoirs through Women's Studies. Once, when her department was being introduced at a campus conference, the president referred to Stella as "our wild librarian." The nickname stuck. Stella didn't mind because she felt it summed her up pretty well.

Through their work on the committee, Stella and Robert became fast friends. Like many others, she could sense a sweet, mysterious ingredient in Robert's personality, and Robert appreciated Stella's fiery, compassionate spirit and what he called her "full throttle" approach to life. It wasn't long before she was invited to dinner at Robert's home to meet Maria. It was the first of many lunches and dinners the three of them would spend together.

Maria had long ago quit her job as a hostess at a popular local restaurant. She kept busy with her newfound talent of pottery, which had developed from several semesters of ceramics at the college. Some days, she met Stella and Robert on campus for lunch still wearing a smock decorated with clay splatter. Dust and particles from her artist life added magic and whimsy to her rich, dark hair. Stella loved being with both of them. She discovered they were a mostly private couple who did little socializing, so she considered her friendship with them a special gift.

Over time, Stella came to know about Maria's miscarriages and how the couple were unable to have children. Although Maria was past the age to bear children, Stella sensed she still struggled with this when she saw Maria's eyes tear up during a conversation. Stella learned how Maria had lost her parents years before and Robert's parents were both elderly and ill with frequent hospitalizations. Stella also shared about some of her past relationships and how she was now happy to be what she called "blissfully single."

"And what is that like?" Maria asked.

"Being single?" Stella looked at Maria.

"Blissfully," Maria said.

"Oh," Stella began. "You know that saying, 'Follow your bliss?' I heard it when I was a much younger woman and took it to heart. I suppose I've just not been so traditional with my desires, and I don't mind being a bit of an oddball." She laughed and continued. "I've always been independent and have enjoyed living on my own. My career as a librarian, teaching, the students, baking, and my love of books and reading have made my life so full."

"That's wonderful," Maria said, looking intently at Stella with a soft smile.

"That doesn't mean I haven't experienced some hard times," Stella said. She revealed the sorrow of the loss of her parents to cancer, but how her close bond with her brother, Ben, who worked as an accountant in Seattle, provided support during the grieving process. She spoke of the daily joy she experienced with her adopted German shepherd Jane and her dream of opening a combination bakery and bookstore to bring her two passions together. By this time, she was planning her exit, as she was thick in her research of opening a small business and following her dream.

"As you probably guessed," she told them, casting her hand up as if making an important declaration, "it will be one hundred percent vegan. As I am."

"Oh no," Robert said, "this part I'm not so sure about."

Stella laughed it away. "Just wait and see. You'll be pleasantly surprised."

"Well, no matter what," Maria said, pointing at Robert, "you will always have one loyal and devoted customer."

"Don't you mean two devoted customers?" Robert asked, pulling

Maria close to him.

Just shy of two years later when Robert came to the grand opening of the bakery to see Stella's dream realized, he delighted in the different book-themed treats. He marveled over the mural designed by a local artist collective that spanned an entire wall and the exquisite built-in floor to ceiling bookshelves expertly crafted by Andy's partner, Alex. They were packed with new and used books organized within a variety of unusual categories: "Love Studies," "California Dreaming," "Wild Women," "Beat Generation," "Magical Vegan Living," "Feminists We Love," "Poets We Love," "Artists We Love," and others devoted to specific writers: Clarissa Pinkola Estés, June Jordan, Mary Oliver, Anais Nin, Thich Nhat Hanh, Alice Walker, and Toni Morrison. Robert even admired the flooring. He kneeled down to place his palm against it.

"It's polished concrete," Stella told him.

"Of course," he said. "Beautiful."

They sat at the community table that first day, and Robert enjoyed his inaugural serving of the beer bread.

"It looks like you really pulled it off, lady!" he said to Stella while making a gesture with his arm, stretching it out to his side as if to capture everything he saw.

"I think so," she said, "but there are still some final pieces I didn't have time to arrange."

She took Robert to an empty shelving unit that was set up where the bakery case ended. "This is being reserved for art by local artists. I'm thinking of a wonderful potter who could sell her creations here. What do you think?" She winked, and of course, Robert knew just who she was thinking of.

The next day, Robert and Maria came in together carrying a large wooden crate. Maria got to work arranging her pottery on the shelves. The items were round, feminine, and sensual, including small lavender vases, creamy turquoise bowls, and multicolored pendants on silver and gold chains. Stella brought them coffee and a plate with a large serving of Poet's Beer Bread.

"Dear God," Robert said with his eyes closed and a smile after taking a few bites, "it's an experience."

Maria pulled a cardboard box onto her lap. "Come sit with us," she said to Stella. "This is for you." Maria smiled as she handed the box to Stella. Wrapped inside luxurious gold tissue paper, Stella's hands revealed a sky-blue bowl with a delicate line of gold around the lip. The very bottom of the exterior was covered in a gentle purple shade. She recognized them as the colors of the Wild Librarian's exterior and front door.

"Oh my," Stella said, turning the bowl around in her hands and feeling how it was perfectly balanced. It had a firm but not oppressive weight. It was hard to find any words as she closed her eyes to settle into the moment.

Stella opened her eyes to find Robert and Maria looking at her. She could tell they were pleased by her reaction. Robert placed his arm around Maria.

"I just love it," Stella said. "Thank you."

"I normally call these my soul bowls," Maria said. "But for you, this is a prosperity bowl."

Maria's pottery quickly became a hit. It was not only beautiful but something unexpected and wonderful to find for sale in a bakery. The location of the pottery shelves near the bakery case also contributed to her success, as her creations became items to admire while customers took in the assortment of baked goods.

A rhythm developed, with Maria coming in every other Wednesday or Thursday afternoon while Robert was taking a swimming class at a local community center. Stella would provide Maria with a check for any items that had sold over the preceding two weeks, and Maria would restock the shelves with new captivating pieces. It wasn't long before some customers asked the bakery staff to get in touch with Maria, leading to her entry into commissioned work.

On one of Maria's Wednesday visits, Stella was arranging copies of Thomas Moore's *Soul Mates* on top of the bakery case. Valentine's

Day was approaching, and the Wild Librarian was taking reservations for themed boxes customers could pick up on the holiday. Each box would include a copy of *Soul Mates* and an assortment of tiny cupcakes.

"Yum!" Maria said to Stella, nodding toward a promotional image of the tiny cupcakes.

"This is our first time trying a holiday-themed box," Stella said.

Maria picked up a copy of *Soul Mates*. "Honoring the mysteries of love and relationship." She read the subtitle out loud.

Stella watched Maria scan through the book and draw her finger down the table of contents.

"Endings. Pathologies of Love," Maria said, reading the titles of some of the chapters. "Stella, are you sure this is a book for Valentine's Day?"

"Well," Stella laughed, "if I remember, those are small parts of the book, but love is a complex thing, right?"

Maria didn't say anything. She turned to a place in the book and read for a minute or so.

"I'll take a copy," she told Stella.

A few days later, Andy was talking with Robert about his swimming class when Stella came into the bakery from the back. It was early, and the morning rush would soon be upon them. Stella smiled when she saw Robert demonstrate something from his class, with his arms quickly going up in the air and then out to his sides.

"Look at you, Robert!" Stella called out. "Becoming an athlete."

Robert laughed and gave a thumbs-up.

As customers started arriving for their morning coffee, Robert took one of his favorite window seats. When it slowed down, Stella came over to him holding two light blue T-shirts.

"What do you think?" she asked. She set the shirts down and then held one up in front of her so Robert could see it. Across the front, it read, "Chocolate before noon," in bold letters. Then, in smaller print below: "At the Wild Librarian Bakery and Bookstore, Santa Ana, California."

Robert clapped his hands together. "Great!" he said.

Stella placed the two shirts near him. "One for you, and one for Maria."

"Aww, thank you, Stella!" He touched the lettering on one of the shirts.

"Is Maria enjoying *Soul Mates*? Has she started it?" Stella asked, pulling out a chair to sit down.

"*Soul Mates?*" Robert looked puzzled, making Stella cringe inside when she realized he may not know about Maria's purchase of the book. She would never have asked such a question at the college library, considering it a violation of a patron's privacy, but here, among friends and thinking Robert and Maria shared so much, the question innocently rolled out. Robert took a sip of his coffee.

"It's a book by Thomas Moore," Stella said.

"I didn't know she was reading it," he said, appearing not to think much of it and moving on to ask Stella her thoughts on a new fine and performing arts complex the college was constructing.

The next time Maria came to the bakery, she was carrying a box of bowls she recently made.

"Oh, how lovely," Stella and Grace said, peering into the box. They were mostly in the shades Stella had come to admire and associate with Maria's pottery—lavender, turquoise, a spectrum of blues—but there were also two larger bowls in a deep red color.

Grace pointed to the red bowls. "I love these."

Maria moved closer with the box, and Grace put her fingers on one of the bowls.

"Ruby red." Maria smiled at Grace.

"They look like they should feel warm," Grace said.

"I guess I was inspired to try something new." Maria laughed.

Stella pulled her attention from the bowls to Maria. Maria's mouth was open wide and her laugh uncharacteristically wild and loud.

As Maria began arranging the bowls, Grace left to assist a customer. Stella stayed with Maria. She hadn't forgotten the recent conversation with Robert.

"Are you enjoying *Soul Mates*?" she asked Maria.

"I am!" Maria said.

"Maria," Stella began, "last week I committed a librarian faux pas."

Maria continued arranging the pottery on the shelves.

"Robert came in for his usual morning coffee and Poet's Bread. I asked him if you were enjoying *Soul Mates*."

Maria stopped and turned toward Stella. "What's wrong with that?" she asked her.

"Well, it was clear Robert didn't know about the book. I feel I violated your privacy, and I'm sorry."

Maria laughed again in that open and free way. "Oh, Stella! You look so concerned! That's not a big deal."

Stella felt relieved. She turned when she heard the front door open and was about to step away when Maria placed a hand firmly on her forearm.

"Stella," she began, keeping her hand in place, "you would need to do something horribly bad to ever offend me." Maria's eyes focused intently on Stella's. "I think you are a truly wonderful person. Don't you ever forget it."

Stella thanked Maria but found her suddenly serious tone odd. She stepped away when Grace called out for assistance.

While explaining about the book collection to a woman with a small child, Stella could still feel the imprint of Maria's grip on her forearm. She looked over the woman's shoulder and saw Maria continuing to arrange her pottery on the shelves. Any seriousness from the previous moment had clearly passed for Maria. Stella saw her moving around as if she were swaying to music, happily humming a tune.

Looking back, Stella could never have imagined what would happen.

It was just a few weeks after the Wild Librarian's second anniversary celebration with the *Los Angeles Times*, the framed photograph from the day's festivities already hanging on the wall in Stella's office, when Stella and Grace were at work early handling preparations for the day. The positive coverage in the paper had increased business for the already successful bakery. They were baking extra Enchanted Lemon Pecan Cupcakes for a large writing group that had reserved several tables for their monthly meeting that morning.

It wasn't yet 6:00 a.m. when the phone rang. Robert was on the line. "Stella!" he yelled. "Thank God I got you. Maria is missing."

Robert had gone to his swimming class the day before. When he returned home, Maria's car wasn't in the driveway. She hadn't mentioned she was going out, but he didn't think much of it at first. After making a late lunch, he called her. He was startled when he heard the familiar ring of her cell phone and found her phone on one of the nightstands next to their bed. Once it got close to the time they usually ate dinner, he was a wreck. He tried to soothe himself with a glass of wine on the back porch. Time slowly ticked away, and then it was 10:00 p.m. Maria was always in bed by then.

Robert had started calling anyone he could think of, including Stella, who was already asleep with her phone turned off. He went out to the garage where Maria had her pottery studio. Everything seemed to be in place. Feeling nervous, he drove around to places they would go—the grocery store, the twenty-four-hour laundromat on Fourth Street, the community center, the bar on Seventeenth Street—frantically scanning around him, looking for her car. He drove by the closed Wild Librarian with a lump starting in his throat. Feeling panicked, by midnight, he drove home and called the police.

Two officers came to see Robert. He let them in, and they assessed the situation. Since Maria had only been missing for a few hours, nothing could be done yet. They recommended he contact hospitals and try to remain calm. After they left, he made several calls that led to nothing. He sat on a chair in the living room, jumping at every sound outside on the street.

Within a few days, the search for Maria occupied much of the city. It seemed everyone knew about it. Flyers were posted all around downtown and beyond in adjacent communities. Guy Mandal even placed a flyer, stapled to thick cardboard, next to him on the park bench while playing his accordion for passersby. All the local television news shows came to film in the area. A call center was set up in a reception room at Holy Family Cathedral. People walked in groups going door-to-door to hand out flyers. Detectives came to the Wild Librarian to ask Stella, Grace, Andy, and others questions. Robert heard they even went to the restaurant Maria had worked at years back.

A detective came to see Robert at home. With Robert's permission, the police looked around the house. They asked him questions, including many of the same ones, over and over. Were there marital problems? Did they recently have a fight? Did they have financial problems? Was there anyone who wanted to harm them? They also had Robert come down to the station, where they put him in an interrogation room. Manuel Clark was the main detective assigned to the case. Robert sat across the table from Detective Clark. They were in an interior room of the police station without windows. Robert couldn't help but feel he had become like a character in one of his Lifetime movies.

"Thank you for coming down," Detective Clark began. He had a yellow legal pad in front of him. "We haven't been able to find any leads." He went through the litany of questions again.

"Did Maria have any enemies?"

"Definitely not."

"Anyone she recently had trouble with?"

"No."

"And she got along with everyone at the studio?" This was a new question.

"The studio?"

"The classroom studio at the college. For her ceramics."

"Oh, it's been a few years since she completed her classes."

"But we understand she still used the studio at times. At least up to a few months ago. We recently discovered she had been given some type of special permission."

Robert started to feel warm. His right leg was shaking. "I wasn't aware of that," he told Detective Clark, feeling as if the ground had shifted a little underneath him. He suddenly felt unsteady and too confused to focus his thoughts. He looked at the door, hoping the detective was almost done and he could leave.

The detective tapped the edge of the legal pad with a pen. "You know, Robert," he began, "sometimes when adults go missing, it's because they don't want to be found. People sometimes just leave."

"No." Robert could feel the sweat gathering above his upper lip. "Not my Maria."

Even though Detective Clark believed Maria might have simply left Robert, considering he'd seen similar cases numerous times in his career there were puzzling elements that continued to bother him and others familiar with the story. Except for Maria's car, her purse seemed to be the only personal item missing from their home. Robert couldn't tell if any clothes or other belongings were missing, but nothing appeared to be. Money hadn't been withdrawn from their bank account. Maria's credit cards hadn't been used. Her cell phone had no activity but for a few incoming calls from telemarketers. Yet no evidence of foul play had been detected.

Groups continued to canvas the area, and the call center was staffed throughout most mornings and afternoons. In just a few days, the story of "the missing woman in California" began to attract national attention. Ben, Stella's brother in Seattle, heard about it through coverage on a community radio station. He called her at home one evening.

"Santa Ana is in the news up here. Do you know the couple?" he asked. "They mentioned the man used to work at your old college."

"Yes—remember Robert, the welding professor you met at the bakery, and his wife who makes the pottery?"

"Oh, God. They were delightful. I hadn't made the connection."

"There's been a flurry of activity here," Stella told him.

"Well, it just goes to show, you never really know what's happening behind closed doors."

"Ben!" Stella admonished him. "I know Robert. There is no way he hurt her."

"I'm not saying that, Stella," Ben said. "That didn't cross my mind. I just think she might have left him. You know. Marital problems."

"I know them well," Stella told him. "Robert is always showering Maria with love. Buying her flowers. Kissing her. Constantly doting on her."

"Hmm. Sounds like Rebecca. Yikes."

Stella rarely thought about Rebecca these days. It had been so many years since Ben left her. Rebecca was Ben's girlfriend throughout college and even after graduation. Everyone assumed they would marry.

"Remember how mad you and Mom were when I ended it with her? Jeez. Such drama!"

Stella definitely remembered. It all came back: Rebecca calling Stella multiple times as she struggled to accept the breakup. Rebecca seeing a psychotherapist. She recalled Ben describing Rebecca's love as "suffocating."

Ben continued. "I remember you said some silly poetic thing to Rebecca that seemed to help. It ended her calls. What was it?"

"It wasn't silly, Ben!" Stella said. "I told her, 'With the right person, your song will sing.'"

"That's right. 'Your song will sing.' My God!"

Stella laughed a little, realizing how it must have sounded to Ben who was kind and caring but not the romantic or poetic type. During one heated argument all those years ago, Stella and her mom had overheard Ben accuse Rebecca of living in a fantasy. As far as Stella knew, things worked out for Rebecca, and her life did sound a bit unreal. She met a Greek musician, married him, and moved to

Greece, where she worked for a travel agency that catered to women going on goddess tours. Stella reflected on Rebecca and sat with Ben's comments for a few seconds. Then she remembered some of the disturbing factors in Maria's disappearance.

"No," Stella told him, "I don't think Maria left Robert. Ben, money hasn't been withdrawn from their bank account."

"Huh, that's odd," Ben said. "Well, it's terribly sad no matter what happened. I hope it's nothing ominous."

After several weeks, the canvassing tapered off and the call center closed. Then it was only down to a few faithful to keep up the efforts.

Maria's disappearance continued to occupy much of Stella's mind. She touched the prosperity bowl Maria had made, which she kept on the nightstand next to her bed. In the dark at night, especially when there was a bright moon and Stella kept her curtains open, the bowl offered a quiet glow. On those nights, when she reached out to touch it, the fine gold line along the lip felt cool against her fingers.

Robert often came into the Wild Librarian to sit with Stella in her office. He would replay certain conversations he'd had with Maria to see if Stella could pick up on any clues. The questions seemed endless. "Do you think she was planning to leave me?" "Do you think there was someone else and he hurt her?" "Could she have suffered some kind of mental breakdown and driven off unaware of what she was doing, and then something terrible happened?" "Was she abducted?" "If she left freely on her own, why?" "Where could she have gone?" He told Stella he didn't know Maria had still been using the studio at the college. "Why wouldn't she have told me?"

"Maybe she did, and you just don't remember. Maybe she didn't go there that much. Robert, it doesn't sound like a big deal."

"But when was she going there that I wouldn't know?"

"Maybe when you were at your swimming class," Stella offered.

"Swimming . . ." Robert said the word quietly. He had been going faithfully twice a week until Maria's disappearance, but it now seemed like something faraway and fanciful that he no longer had any interest in.

As time passed and the media attention waned, Stella formed a part of a core group with a few of Robert's former colleagues and students who continued to place fresh flyers around town. She kept a flyer posted on the window of the Wild Librarian and another near the cash register. Robert occasionally heard from Detective Clark. Sightings came in from random places—Boulder, Colorado; Sedona, Arizona; Richmond, Virginia—but they never panned out. The names of the cities haunted Robert's imagination. He kept a list of them in a small spiral-bound notepad he started to carry with him everywhere. It was the type of notepad he'd used in an earlier life while out on construction sites. He was unable to sleep without a medication prescribed by his doctor.

Robert kept everything in his house just as it had been the night Maria disappeared. The crossword puzzle from the Sunday paper that she was working on took up part of the couch. The empty glass she drank from was on the coffee table. He dusted around these and other objects, careful not to move them. His superstitious mind believed she might return if everything stayed in its place.

When he wasn't at the Wild Librarian, hanging up flyers, or trying to sleep or eat, Robert would often sit at the small table in his kitchen. He always found the four chairs circling the table uncomfortable and had wanted to get rid of them for quite some time, but now he found their odd structure a thing of value. It was nearly impossible to get lazy in such uncomfortable chairs. They aided him in staying alert.

The chair with its back closest to the tiny kitchen window was the one Maria liked to sit in. One night, Robert sat in her chair. He took in the room from that angle. He could see much more than he could from his usual spot. There was the old refrigerator, the small toaster oven on the counter, the Mr. Coffee pot that seemed almost as old as their marriage, and a framed embroidery Maria had made years ago. It was the only one he remembered her ever making, featuring two calico cats and a black cat surrounded by yellow daisies. The embroidery seemed like a trite creation in comparison to her luminous clay pieces. Looking at it made Robert sad. He remembered it had seemed to take her a long time to finish it. He wanted to ask her about it and why she only made this one. Then he saw her handmade apron hanging on a hook where the cabinets ended. Like the embroidery, it had been her first and last attempt at sewing. Both were so different from making pottery, which seemed to grab a hold of her from her first class. He realized he had never asked her about that. What was it about ceramics that held her interest so well?

Against the back of his neck, Robert felt a cool breeze coming through the screen of the tiny window. He got up and moved to the living room.

It was two months after Maria's disappearance when a new sighting was reported. Robert didn't find out from the police, but from a tabloid news show he'd started to watch habitually. The show was sensationalist, with stories of crimes, celebrities, and missing people dominating the short segments. It had devoted many episodes to Maria's story when she first went missing. Even though he didn't know them, Robert felt a connection to the family members of other missing people who were interviewed on the show, especially the husbands. Their shared suffering, the long blackness of unknowing they all navigated in, gave him minutes of relief from his loneliness and despair.

He was watching one night when a banner flashed across the bottom of the screen along with the usual dramatic music. It read, "New sighting of missing California woman." He leaned forward to hear the manicured blonde woman begin the segment. "Could it be that after going missing from her Santa Ana home nearly one year ago, Maria Gonzales has been found?" Robert could feel his heart pounding in his ears. He discovered there had been a "potentially positive sighting" at a bookstore in Berkeley.

Robert searched on his phone and found the bookstore mentioned on the tabloid show. It closed at 5:00 p.m. He checked the time. 7:20 p.m. He still called. Maybe someone was working late.

The phone rang and rang. He imagined how it sounded in the dark silence with all the books around. He hung up and ran his comb through his hair. He called again. Same thing.

Robert thought of Detective Clark. Should he call the police station? Clark would already be gone for the day, so there was no point, but he felt he needed to share this information with someone who would understand the importance.

It was a Tuesday night. The Wild Librarian would still be open. He thought it may be the week when Stella met with her book club. Instead of calling first, he got in his truck and drove there. He found street parking around the corner and walked briskly down the sidewalk. His chest was pounding. He felt lightheaded. He opened the door and scanned the interior until he saw Stella at a large table with a group of women. He recognized a few of them who had helped post flyers of Maria. One was Mary Chin. And Elly Kim.

As he headed for the table, a voice called out, "Robert, hello. How are you?" It was Mrs. McDaniels. He hadn't noticed the McDaniels sitting near the bookshelves. They were at a small table, their knees almost touching underneath. Their bodies swallowed up the chairs.

"I'm here to see Stella," he said, sounding out of breath. "There's been a new sighting. A sighting of Maria."

"Oh!" they both said, their eyebrows moving up in unison. Eleanor McDaniels gripped the top of her walking stick resting against her leg, and Frank McDaniels nodded.

Robert turned and made his way across the room. His appearance at the table made the women in the book club look up.

"Robert," Mary Chin said, "are you here to join us?"

"There's been a new sighting," he told them. Two women who were at the bakery for the first time weren't sure what this meant, but they sensed the drama.

"Oh, Robert!" Stella said. Her face was serious, and her eyes were hopeful. She stood up. "Where?"

"A bookstore in Berkeley. It's called University Press Books."

"I know the place," Stella said. "It's right by the campus. How did you find out? Does Detective Clark know?" She made a gesture toward her office and told the women to carry on without her.

Robert told Stella all he knew from the TV episode and how he had called the store but no one answered. "They open at ten tomorrow," he said. Before Robert even told her, Stella knew he would soon be on his way.

Robert tried to rest in preparation for the drive up north, but he mostly lay in bed with the hallway light on, staring at the ceiling. He left before 5:00 a.m. the next morning to beat the traffic. By 6:00 a.m., he was already cruising past downtown Los Angeles and making good time through the San Fernando Valley. He took the 5, the straightest line to the Bay Area, only stopping once in Fresno County to fill up his gas tank.

He walked a few large circles around the lot at the gas station, looking out into the expansive fields around him. There was a distant scent of cow manure. He went into the convenience market to get coffee and something to eat then drove the next few miles while eating a breakfast burrito and taking sips of a large black coffee. The burrito hadn't been heated thoroughly in the microwave, so some bites were hot, and others were lukewarm. Robert, fueled by hope and adrenaline, had no idea how exhausted his mind and body were or that the sauce from the burrito had dripped onto his sweater and puddled here and there.

He found a talk radio station to listen to for a stretch. An author was talking about his book, a fictional work inspired by the Pacific Ocean. He commented on how his family had moved from the Texas Panhandle to the central California coast when he was a small child. The move was hard for them at first. He described it as a "cultural adjustment." They spent their weekends going to the beach, and this helped them with the transition since one thing they were enamored by was living so close to the ocean. The husband and wife in his book were based on his parents. "They had something that almost seems miraculous to me now, as an adult," the author said. "A very happy marriage. Of course, I don't know the inner workings of it all, but I never remember them having an argument." Robert felt the beginning of a nervous stirring. "They were married for over fifty years," the author continued with his confident, even-tempered voice, "and died within six months of each other. My mother first—"

Robert turned off the radio.

He reached Berkeley in the early afternoon. It was still lunchtime, so the traffic was congested as he made his way through the city and down University Avenue. He used the GPS on his phone to find the Bancroft Hotel, where he had a room reserved for that night. The hotel was on a street of the same name—Bancroft Way—and sat directly across from the UC Berkeley campus. Students were everywhere. On the sidewalks. In the crosswalks. Robert found the small lot next to the hotel. When he called the night before, the hotel clerk had told him he could keep his truck there during his stay. An old attendant in a little booth opened a sliding door to get Robert's name and hand him a parking pass. Although it wasn't cool out, the attendant wore a wrinkled tan trench coat. It made Robert think of the Columbo character from the old detective series.

Robert's room barely had enough space for the bed, nightstand, and upholstered chair. It was so tiny he wondered how it could be as expensive as it was, but he didn't linger too much on these thoughts since he had made it to Berkeley, and soon he would be at University Press Books. He took the change of clothes he'd brought and a small case of toiletries out of his traveling bag, placing them near the foot of the bed. He set a take-out container from the Wild Librarian on the nightstand. Inside was a large serving of Poet's Beer Bread that Stella had insisted he take with him. He left a notepad, pen, digital camera, and flyers about Maria inside the bag. Then he washed his face and hands in the tiny sink in the tiny bathroom and used one of the tiny white washcloths that had an odd, awful smell to dry off.

He started down Bancroft Way toward University Press Books with his bag slung over his right shoulder. The campus stayed with him on his right side as he walked several blocks. There were tennis courts and grand buildings. Everything was bustling about him—people, cars, buses, dogs. It was a pleasant spring day, so the windows of the cafes and restaurants he passed were open. Music and loud voices came out onto the sidewalk. The life of the city added more drama to Robert's agenda.

It was easy to find the bookstore. It was so easy, in fact, that Robert wondered if things were becoming aligned. Was he reaching an end to his suffering? Was he about to receive an answer?

Before he got to the door, he saw the clerk at the cashier stand through the glass window. He wore horn-rimmed glasses and had a nicely trimmed beard. He was middle-aged. Robert felt reassured. The clerk looked like someone who would take the matter seriously.

Robert opened the door. It was an old, heavy wooden door that required a bit of a push. A bell hanging around the knob rattled. He approached the clerk. The counter was higher than most store counters and appeared to be made from thick wood like the door. It reminded Robert of where a judge would sit in a courtroom.

"I'm Robert Gonzales from Santa Ana," he told the clerk. He added the name of the college where he had taught welding as if this might add more of an official tone to his visit.

The clerk nodded but didn't say anything. Robert's hair was disheveled and he was still unaware of the food stains on his sweater from the earlier breakfast burrito. Berkeley was full of odd people, and most days at least a few ventured in off the street, so the clerk waited to see what would happen next before taking any action.

"You see, I drove up here from Santa Ana because my wife is missing. She's been missing for nine months. She was recently seen here at this store." Robert pulled a flyer with Maria's photograph from his traveling bag and handed it to the clerk.

"Yes," the clerk said, "I know about this. A film crew were here earlier in the week. They made a mess of the place. Took us most of the day to clean up after them and get things back in order."

Robert waited to hear more.

"I told them I didn't recognize the missing woman. What I mean is—forgive me—I'm sorry, but I don't recognize your wife. I can't say I ever saw her."

"What about others?" Robert asked. "Other people who work here. Customers?"

"Sir, I'm sorry. The owner shared a picture of your wife with all of us when we received a call from that news show. None of us recall seeing her. The owner told the show this, but they still insisted on coming."

"And customers?"

"Well, there's no way to ask every customer. How would we ever find them? If you'd like to leave this flyer, I'm sure we can put it in the window."

Robert wasn't sure what to do next. He zipped his bag shut to protect the contents and moved his head to the side to take in the bookstore. It wasn't much larger than his living room. He made a comment about wanting to look around as he shuffled toward the back of the store. He found chairs arranged around a large table.

Robert sat down. He dug around in his traveling bag, pulling out a pen and his small notepad. He turned to the pages with the list he'd made titled "Cities with Sightings" and wrote the date, time, and name of the bookstore before getting up and making his way back near the front. He noticed a few stairs leading to a small, elevated alcove filled with more books. It was an elegant and mysterious space. Robert heard classical music. He noticed a cutout in the wall. The music was coming from there. He looked through, discovering a cafe on the other side. He could smell the coffee and food. The aroma mingled with the stacks of used books in front of him, reminding him of the Wild Librarian, and he felt a pull deep inside his chest. He wanted to like what he was taking in—it had the qualities of romance he had always enjoyed—but almost as soon as he felt the pull, there was that new sensation that had been with him since Maria disappeared. It was a hollowness. If he put his hand on his chest, he could move his fingers around and find the exact place where the hollowness emanated from.

"Sir? Mr. Gonzales?" It was the clerk coming up to the alcove. "I just thought of something."

Robert was pulled back into the bookstore. He remembered the long drive and that he was in Berkeley.

"Maybe your wife was spotted at another bookstore close by and the person remembered wrong. There are several bookstores within walking distance."

Robert handed his notepad to the clerk and asked him to write down the information. Leaving University Press Books behind, he headed first to Half Price Books, then East Wind, and back up Telegraph Avenue to Moe's and Shakespeare and Co. He stopped at a new age-type bookstore. He walked down College Avenue to inquire at Mrs. Dalloway's. It was the same everywhere he went. The people were genuinely concerned, accepting flyers of Maria to hang up, but no one recalled seeing her.

Back at the Bancroft in the evening, Robert sat up in bed eating the Poet's Beer Bread. It was dark in his room except for the light from the television. He heard voices walking down the hallway outside his door. It sounded as if someone in the group was tapping something along the floor. He thought of Eleanor McDaniels' walking stick. Robert took one of the pills his doctor had prescribed. In the morning, he would begin his drive home.

It was difficult to see Robert in the weeks following his return from Berkeley. Something about the journey had set a finality in his stomach that felt like a weighted ball. This weight could be seen in his eyes. When he came into the bakery, he created a gravity—an intensity that made the typical joys of daily life and small talk stop until he left. The sorrow of the situation and who Robert had become settled over the bakery staff and regular customers who knew him and his story. But over time, everyone discovered a new way to interact with him. Life, as it does, carried on. The normal sounds and chatter continued even with his appearances, but, of course, everyone remembered what had happened, and it was the first thing they thought of whenever they saw him.

Not too long after Maria's disappearance, Stella moved her pottery to the bakery stockroom to keep the leftover pieces safe in a cardboard box. She didn't feel comfortable continuing to sell the pieces in Maria's absence, but she also didn't want to ask Robert about something that seemed minuscule compared to what he was dealing with. If Robert noticed Stella moved them, he didn't say anything.

When she felt enough time had passed after his drive to Berkeley, Stella asked Robert to come to the storeroom when he came in one day.

"I put Maria's pottery back here," she explained. "The pieces that didn't sell yet."

He took the box from Stella. "This is all?" He turned to look around at the supply racks and a large built-in cabinet full of boxes and various items along one wall.

"Yes. Everything else sold."

"I assumed there was more being stored back here, maybe to rotate the shelves, considering how much she made."

"Her items sold quickly. As you know, her work was greatly admired." Stella saw Robert's face turn from curious to perplexed.

"I guess I didn't realize how much," he said.

"Why, yes," Stella told him. "And of course, the commissioned pieces were never held here for long or at all if Maria made other arrangements."

"Commissioned pieces?"

Stella began to feel uncomfortable as she realized she was unintentionally revealing secrets she didn't know she possessed. But a door had been opened, and Robert stood in front of her waiting.

"Several customers commissioned pieces beyond the vases for Luna's," she explained.

"Vases for Luna's? You mean the restaurant next door?" Lines appeared between Robert's eyebrows as his face shifted, and his voice tapered off as if he were speaking to himself.

"You clearly didn't know any of this," Stella said, her voice soft and concerned as she looked at Robert still holding the box against his chest. She thought of how Maria had come in alone twice a month to bring new pieces, rearrange her pottery, and collect any funds while Robert was at his swimming class. She'd never thought anything of it. She considered that with the commissioned pieces for Luna's and other customers, Maria must have made thousands of dollars Robert wasn't aware of. They stood in silence, hearing the sounds of the bakery in the distance, as pieces of a puzzle knitted together in their minds.

After a long pause, Robert broke the silence. "Thank you, Stella. I'll take these home."

As he passed by Luna's Italian Restaurant on the way to his truck, Robert looked through the windows. On each table, he saw one of the elegant cream-colored vases Maria used to make. He tried to remember what she told him when he saw her packing the vases up in several boxes. Had she said they were donations for a charity organization? He couldn't recall her exact words, but he knew she had lied.

Robert returned home and carried the box of pottery from the Wild Librarian out to the garage where Maria had her studio. He saw several of her smocks hanging near the worktable. He pressed his face into one of the smocks, inhaling any remaining traces of her fragrance, and replayed the conversation with Stella. Although he was standing in his own home, a nervousness filled him that felt similar to being in the interrogation room with Detective Clark. He pushed his face deeper into the fabric as his eyes teared up. Robert stood motionless as he sobbed, trying to catch his breath. He grabbed the smock tightly, causing him to feel something like thick paper crumpling in his hand. Looking down, he discovered a business card in the front pocket. It was Malcolm Boyd's card from the college. He had been Maria's ceramics professor. There was a phone number written on the back. Robert's hand shook as he pulled his cell phone from his pocket. He sat on Maria's tall stool in front of the worktable and dialed the number.

"Tony's," a man's voice said.

"What is this?" Robert asked.

"Excuse me?" the man yelled over clamor in the background.

"Where have I called?"

"This is Tony's Bar and Grill."

Robert searched his mind to try to find a connection. He didn't know the place. "Where are you located?"

"Long Beach. On PCH."

Robert hung up. He stood, looking around the garage at Maria's tools and containers. He turned the business card back over and dialed the number for Malcolm Boyd's office, but when he reached the voice mail for a different faculty member, he hung up. Robert's body felt tense. He considered it wasn't odd to find Boyd's business card. After all, he was Maria's professor; she may have worn the smock while in his class. He felt pulled toward something though, as if after being lost, he was starting to make his way through a dense fog.

Robert got back on his phone and called the main line for the college. He asked for the art department, hoping to get Boyd's number from the secretary. He remembered finding his boisterous manner and Scottish accent overbearing when their paths occasionally crossed at faculty meetings.

"Oh, hi, Robert." A woman's voice sounded on the other end of the line. "I'm not sure if you remember me. We were on an awards committee together."

Robert was polite, but he wasn't up for small talk or reminiscing. "I'm trying to get a hold of Malcolm Boyd. I called his office phone, but it went through to someone else."

"Malcolm, yes. He retired last year. We've sure lost some good ones lately." Her voice was chipper.

"I'd like to get a hold of him."

"Sure, sure. Hold on a moment. I don't think I have a new phone number handy since his move, but I have his personal email."

"He moved?"

"Yes, yes. He lived for so many years in Long Beach, then he up and left almost right after his retirement. To Walnut Creek. I think his family has property there."

"Walnut Creek. Is that out in Riverside or San Bernardino?"

"Oh, no. It's up in the Bay Area. You know, next to Berkeley. I hear it's very nice."

The names of the cities whirled around in Robert's head. Long Beach, the location of the place called Tony's, and of course, Berkeley. He saw himself standing inside University Press Books and remembered the terrible smell of the washcloth at the Bancroft Hotel. His stomach began to churn.

He hung up and started rummaging through boxes Maria had stacked up on a shelf above her workspace. He'd looked through these boxes before, as he had done extensively throughout the house, searching for clues. This time felt different. He could sense the business card where he'd placed it in his front pocket as if it carried heat and felt the usual despair, but there was a slight turning toward suspicion and even a tinge of anger. He began to feel like an animal as he shuffled through one box that was mostly full of tools and a few containers of glaze. He moved to a second that was stuffed with unglazed coffee mugs. Then he reached the third box. It only contained books. He wondered if he had skipped this box before when he saw its contents. He turned it over, and an assortment of paperbacks fell onto the worktable. On top was Thomas Moore's *Soul Mates*. He stared at the title. Then he remembered Stella's question that day. It was something like, "Is Maria enjoying *Soul Mates*?"

Robert carried *Soul Mates* inside. He sat at the small table in the kitchen and opened the book to the first page. He read a few lines then held the book up and began flipping through it until he came to a section titled "Closeness and Distance in Relationship." Several passages had been highlighted in yellow. Did Maria even own a highlighter? He couldn't recall her using one, but he started to feel more uneasy as he read a highlighted sentence about how one person may feel more emotion than the other in a relationship. He came across other highlighted passages, including a section about accepting one's inner mysteries even if they do not fully understand the meaning, and another about how the ending of a relationship can be as mysterious as when the relationship began. The hollow place in his chest was pounding.

"Could it be . . .?" he said out loud, but he couldn't finish the question. Then he tried again. "Could it be . . .?" But the pounding became faster, so he stopped and pushed the book against the hollow place. It was only hours later in bed, as he lay there awake in the dark, that he was able to complete his question. "Could it be that she simply left me for someone else? Could it be that she no longer loved me?"

Robert stayed in bed fully clothed until early afternoon the next day. He started to wonder if the long stretch of despair he had endured since Maria's disappearance was causing him to be overly suspicious. He tossed various scenarios around in his mind. The business card and Boyd's move near Berkeley could simply be a coincidence. And the book? He considered it could have been a used copy and the highlighted passages were not even Maria's. Still, he couldn't get out from under a sinking feeling.

When he stood, finally getting his body up, he felt dizzy. He made his way to the kitchen to make a pot of coffee. He saw *Soul Mates* where he'd left it on the table the night before. It seemed like a book Maria and he could have read together and discussed, but he was beginning to question his own reality. He was tired. He looked down at the pad of paper on the counter and saw the email address for Malcolm Boyd. It seemed so long ago that he'd called the art department secretary, but it had been less than twenty-four hours. Robert placed a call to Detective Clark.

Considering how long it had sometimes taken Robert to get responses from the detective when he'd called about possible sightings in the past, Robert was shocked to get a call the following morning. It was now his second day without any sleep.

"Robert," Detective Clark began, "do you have time to come into the station this morning?"

Robert placed his hand over the hollow place, but it wasn't pounding as it had been. He was surprisingly calm. "Just tell me," he said.

The line was quiet for a few seconds. Robert could hear what sounded like a typewriter in the background. He found it odd yet comforting to hear an old familiar sound from the past.

"Robert," Clark began.

Robert heard a door close on the other end of the line, and he could no longer hear the typing. He saw the detective's small office in his mind. It was a place he had been to many times. He imagined Clark walking from the door to get to his desk. He thought of the gray exterior of the police station surrounded by dirty concrete barriers. It was a depressing place to walk up to that resembled both a drab, lifeless office building and a prison.

"There's no easy way to say this," he continued. "To be frank, I didn't believe what you shared would amount to anything. We got in touch with the Walnut Creek Police Department. They went out to Malcolm Boyd's house. Maria is living there of her own free will."

Robert had been standing. He walked over to the couch to sit down. Next to him was Maria's half-finished crossword puzzle. He placed it in a basket next to the coffee table.

"You talked to her?" he asked.

"No, but the Walnut Creek officers did. They conclusively identified her. I have a photograph I can show you."

"A photograph of Maria?"

"Yes. Taken this morning. Would you like to see it?"

Robert closed his eyes. Maria was alive. A feeling of relief filled him at the same time as anger at her betrayal. It was hard to reconcile the two. He felt he might be sick. He saw Maria in his mind. It was the younger Maria he envisioned from their early years together.

Detective Clark remained on the silent line waiting for Robert's response.

"Yes," Robert said, "I want to see it."

☕

Robert brought a print-out of the photograph to the Wild Librarian later that day. He sat with Stella in her office while she studied the image as if it might reveal some other clues, but it didn't offer much. Maria was standing in a doorway. The tips of wind chimes were visible in the background behind her head.

As Stella learned about Maria living with Malcolm Boyd, she remembered that day at Robert's campus retirement party when she'd overheard Boyd's question about Robert: "Why is he loved so much?" Had Maria told Malcolm things about Robert that no one else knew?

"I think of everything," Robert told Stella, sitting across from her in her office. "All the searching. My notebook full of meaningless clues. Driving up to Berkeley. Just all the hours, days, weeks, months spent. I feel like a fool." He inhaled, filling his lungs with air and letting out an audible exhale. "It's funny," he continued. "You'd think I would jump in my truck and drive up to Walnut Creek to demand an explanation and even try to win her back in some way, but something closed inside me." Even as he said it, Robert felt the hollow place in his chest being covered over. It was still there, but no longer exposed. He believed it was better this way. The closing of the hollow place gave him a sense of protection.

The news was hard for Stella. Of course, she was glad to know Maria was alive, but the betrayal stung. Considering her own feelings, she could not begin to imagine how Robert felt. Yet she couldn't help but also recall all the happy times she'd spent with Maria and Robert. There must have been truth as well in that happiness.

As time passed, Stella continued to feel conflicted. She was angry with Maria, especially for the broken heart and pain Robert now carried, but she couldn't hate her. She found it hard to find words to comfort Robert. She thought of what she'd said to Ben's ex-girlfriend—"With the right person, your song will sing"—but those were words she'd spoken to a young woman after the ending of a relationship of just five or so years. It didn't compare to this.

The story ended for the media too after Maria was located in Walnut Creek. A brief article in the newspaper offered some information through an interview with Detective Clark and unnamed sources claiming Maria had planned to contact Robert shortly after she left. She was startled when she stopped near Santa Barbara and couldn't find her phone. She was "not mentally well" and so continued her drive. Once she reached Walnut Creek and had access to Boyd's phone, she stalled. "I was cowardly and an emotional mess" was a quote attributed to her. Then she heard of the media frenzy. Panicked, she did nothing. "I felt guilty. I had a breakdown." An unnamed source said Maria didn't want to hurt Robert. "She was struggling in their marriage. He wasn't." Stella believed there were parts of the story that she may never fully know. She looked at the framed photograph on her office wall from the second anniversary celebration in the *Los Angeles Times*. It offered much more to contemplate after all the developments since that day. There was Robert holding onto Maria while her hands remained in her lap. To viewers, it might simply appear as a man in love with his arms around his partner. Stella wondered how Robert's arms had felt to Maria that day.

Stella was handling book orders in her office one evening a few weeks after the news broke of Maria living with Malcolm Boyd. She had her dog, Jane, with her when Andy appeared in the doorway to tell her Robert was there. Jane welcomed Robert with a happy howl and an exuberant tail wag before curling back up near the door. Stella and Robert sat at the small table and chairs she had set up across from her desk. She waited for Robert to begin.

"Stella," he started, "there's something about me that I never share with anyone. Only Maria knows. It might seem silly, but I'd like to tell you."

"Okay," Stella said. Through the door, she could hear Andy and Grace beginning to clean things up for the night. They were listening to the classic rock station as they worked.

Robert let a small smile appear—something Stella rarely saw

lately. Then he looked a bit sheepish as he began. "I was a big fan of those made-for-television movies on cable stations. Lifetime and Hallmark channels. I used to also read romance novels like nobody's business."

"I remember seeing them around your home!" Stella said.

"Yeah, but you probably didn't think they were mine, huh?"

"I never gave it too much thought, but I suppose you're right."

"Maria used to tease me. It was our secret. She called me a closet romantic." Robert ran his hand through his thinning hair. "I've stopped it all," he said. "The movies. The novels."

"I can understand why you would stop," Stella told him.

"Yeah. The thing is," he continued, "I wonder if I was living in a fantasy world. You know how the saying goes about 'rose-colored glasses.'" Robert rubbed his eyes with both hands before continuing. Stella noticed he was no longer wearing his wedding band. "I still don't sleep enough," he told her. "I felt young up until the moment she disappeared. I'm now old and tired. I wonder if I will ever be able to retrieve some of my life from before." He sighed and paused. "How does one move on when a major part of your life stopped on a certain day, but you're still alive?"

Stella waited until she thought he was done speaking. He placed his palms on the table while moving back in his chair. "Robert," she said, "I hope one day you get answers, and you find a way to understand and heal. You have been through so much. I don't know what I can do or say, but I'm here. So many of us care deeply for you. Grace. Andy. Alex. Others." Stella looked intently at Robert, taking in his features, seeing how the corners of his mouth now drooped. His face had more lines. It all matched his tired gait.

"I expect the divorce papers any day now."

"I was wondering about that," Stella said. "I'm so sorry."

"She asked to speak with me several times." He looked up quickly at Stella. "But I can't. I just can't."

"I wish you could, Robert."

"I thought you would say that." Robert offered a hint of a smile. "I'm not as brave as you think I am." He closed his eyes. "And it's not just that," he said. "She could have done this another way. She could have left a note, called me the next day, not abandon me so cowardly. I'm not ready to hear her excuses." He leaned back as his eyes filled with tears.

Stella took Robert's hands in hers, and they sat there for several minutes without speaking, surrounded by the comforting and familiar sounds of the bakery closing for the night.

Robert continued to come into the bakery often. He still left hefty tips. At times, he even seemed to enjoy the Poet's Beer Bread and other baked goods. He asked Stella for recommendations from the Wild Librarian's collection and purchased a few titles, which he sat and read at one of his favorite window seats. Stella never gave up hope for Robert to overcome, heal, and become a perhaps quieter version of his old self. His body carried a shadow of his former robust ways that she and a few others could still see.

Stella wondered where Robert would spend his time if the Wild Librarian didn't exist. She supposed the world would offer up another place, but would it have the perfect mix of love, comfort, acceptance, and community for a lost soul like him?

Poet's Beer Bread
Recipe for 1 loaf, 8 mini loaves, or 12 regular-size muffins

3 cups unbleached organic flour
1 teaspoon organic cinnamon
1/2 cup organic raw sugar
1 organic apple, finely chopped
1 tablespoon baking powder
12-ounce bottle of beer*
1 teaspoon salt
1 tablespoon melted vegan butter

Preheat oven to 375 degrees. Whisk together all the dry ingredients Pour in the beer. The batter will get sticky. Knead the batter with your hands for a few seconds to work out most of the lumps. Add the chopped apple pieces. (You can always experiment with the recipe and try adding chopped nuts or raisins!) Dump the batter into mini loaf pans (if you have them) or one regular loaf pan or muffin cups. The loaf pan will take 55–60 minutes, with the smaller versions taking approximately 25 minutes. When the bread is almost done, pour the vegan butter over the top and bake for 5 more minutes. Yum, yum!

*For a recipe without beer, you may try 12 ounces of ginger ale, apple juice or apple cider.

This recipe is adapted from Ashley Rowe's wonderful *Barefoot and in the Kitchen: Vegan Recipes for You.*

PERFECT PAIRING: The world of poetry awaits! And it's so diverse and full of surprises like each bite of this magical bread. Stella recommends diving into some Anne Sexton or Gary Snyder. Try flipping through a large anthology and reading the first poem you open to. You could also seek poetry recommendations from a wild librarian at your local library. There is always at least one on staff!

Enchanted Lemon Pecan Cupcakes
Recipe for 12 regular-size or 6 jumbo cupcakes

1 1/2 cups unbleached organic flour
1 large organic lemon
1 cup organic raw sugar
6 tablespoons organic oil
1/2 cup organic chopped pecans
1 teaspoon organic white vinegar
1 teaspoon baking soda
1 teaspoon organic vanilla extract
water

Preheat oven to 350 degrees. Mix flour, sugar, and baking soda. Grate the lemon rind into a separate measuring cup. Cut the lemon open and squeeze all the juice into the measuring cup. Add water to the measuring cup until you have 1 cup filled. Add this lemon juice concoction to the dry ingredients you already mixed. Add oil, vanilla, and vinegar. Once mixed well, stir in the chopped pecans. Pour batter into your baking cups. Ready to bake! Bake for 18–22 minutes. To make sure the cupcakes are ready, insert a toothpick near the center of one. If the toothpick comes out clean, you know they are done! If any batter sticks to the toothpick, they need to bake for longer. When cool, top with vanilla frosting.

Vanilla Frosting

Use an electric mixer to combine 3/4 cup organic powdered sugar, 3/4 cup softened vegan butter, 2 tablespoons organic almond milk, and 1/4 teaspoon organic vanilla extract. Keep mixing until it is the thickness you desire.

PERFECT PAIRING: Naturally, Thomas Moore's *The Re-enchantment of Everyday Life* goes well with this lemony delight. Wear something comfy. Be prepared to drift off and daydream.

Women and Wolves

It was the fourth Tuesday evening of the month, so The Women Who Run With the Wolves Book Club was gathering at one of the larger tables inside the Wild Librarian. The local jazz radio station was playing lightly through the stereo system, and an aroma of freshly ground coffee, sweet spices, and baked goods filled the space, along with the familiar and comforting scent regular visitors had come to recognize as the many well-loved used books that were mixed in with equal amounts of new books for sale on the floor to ceiling bookshelves. It had been an unusual Southern California day with rain, clouds, and crisp air, so stepping into the heated, aromatic, warmly lit space was especially nice. Extremes in weather always seemed to heighten the fragrance of the books.

Stella came out from behind the counter to greet the book club with a silver tray of just-baked Coconut Jazz Muffins sprinkled with their signature shredded coconut and raw sugar. When she first created these muffins, the rich and sweet flavor of the coconut milk blended with shredded coconut flakes, vanilla, cinnamon, and other ingredients had made her think of Toni Morrison's novels and all the deep layers to her storytelling. Opening a Toni Morrison novel was like biting into a perfectly seasoned muffin with elements of delicious surprise. In her mind, she had run through some of her favorite Morrison novels—*Beloved, Sula, Song of Solomon*—until (of course!) she arrived at *Jazz*. Andy was just a few steps behind her with a dozen Wild Women Blueberry Muffins, named and inspired by the writer and Jungian psychoanalyst Clarissa Pinkola Estés, which were a staple for the book club.

From the day's humidity, Stella's golden hair was especially puffy, curling and twisting up and around her face in different directions. When she was young, her mom had found it nearly impossible to tame young Stella's tangled web, so she often surrendered and affectionately called it her daughter's halo. By the time she was in her forties, Stella had also surrendered. Now in her fifties, her hair was as wild and free as when she was in grade school. She was wearing a pair of her faded blue jeans, a tattered T-shirt, and long earrings with turquoise crescent moons dangling within her hair.

"Ahhhh!" Elly Kim called out when she saw Stella and Andy approaching with the trays. "The jazz muffins! Oh, and our blueberry muffins too!"

Several hands reached up to quickly claim one of each.

Grace walked over with a pad and pen. "Okay, wild ladies! Let me get your drink orders before you start."

The Women Who Run With the Wolves Book Club was the only recurring event at the bakery that Stella not only ran but was an integral member of. It was also the longest running. Enamored by the work of Clarissa Pinkola Estés, the writer of many beloved creations, including the classic *Women Who Run With the Wolves: Myths and Stories of the Wild Woman Archetype,* Stella looked forward every month to the club's gathering to discuss the work of Estés that seemed to provide an infinite number of portals into the women's imaginations and real-life experiences. They discussed creativity and dreams and analyzed the folktales Dr. Estés introduced them to. Stella always made sure the Wild Librarian had a well-stocked supply of Dr. Estés' books for sale. It was an area of the bakery bookstore she especially enjoyed tidying up, dusting, and highlighting.

Membership in the book club would dip and then pick up only to dip again, but a core group of women in their fifties and sixties developed after the first six months and was almost always present.

This included Elly Kim, a poet and writer from Long Beach; Barbara Perez and Sheila Washington, a retired couple who came the whole way from Santa Monica each month; and Mary Chin, a Santa Ana therapist with a successful private practice. They welcomed new and returning members who would pop in from time to time, but they were also perfectly happy to just hang out in their small circle.

Before their retirement, Barbara and Sheila had been high-school teachers for Los Angeles Unified. Barbara taught theatre, and Sheila taught English. This eclectic mix of a poet and writer, librarian-turned-bakery owner, theatre teacher, therapist, and English teacher created many lively discussions. Their life stories were also profoundly different. Like Stella, Elly was single and lived alone in her small home. She had twin daughters with successful careers. One lived in San Francisco, and the other lived in Portland. In her early thirties, Mary lost her husband to a tragic car accident when they were only five years into the makings of a strong and happy marriage. She never remarried and didn't have children. She lived a mostly private and peaceful life with Dr. Freud, her beloved tuxedo cat. Venturing out to join a community group of women was uncharacteristic for Mary, but like Stella, she was a longtime admirer of Estés' work, and she was too curious of something so specific and related to her personal interests not to give it a try. Barbara and Sheila had busy family lives now that they were retired. For most of their marriage, they'd raised Barbara's three sons from her previous marriage. They now had three grandchildren.

Sometimes, the five women would just sit, talk, and laugh for long stretches about their lives, going off on tangents that took them far from the month's selected reading. This feeling of female friendship and the deep sharing of their personal lives was exactly what Stella realized she had wanted when she formed the group. Such deep engagement was new for Mary, who had mostly had lightweight friendships and acquaintances through her professional life over the years. She found it added joy and anticipation to her life that she surprisingly welcomed. Sometimes, when it was just the five of them, they would squeeze together in Stella's office near the back of the Wild Librarian. Elly especially liked the office gatherings, telling the others it felt like a "sacred, secretive space." "Dr. E would approve," she told them, using the shortened version of Estés name they sometimes said as if she were someone they knew well.

After over a year together, when they realized they were the core crew of the discussion group, they organically became a sort of offshoot or, as Sheila called their small team, "a task force." Although it was unspoken, everyone intuitively knew to keep this side collective a secret from others who joined them at times for the monthly discussions.

On this particular night, when the weather in Southern California was atypically rainy, cloudy, and crisp, an exciting and wonderful thought came to Stella. She moved her toes around in her construction boots—a habit of hers when she felt exhilarated or anxious. Realizing it was already ten past the hour and just the five-member task force was present, she rather casually offered to the others: "We should take this club on the road. Travel somewhere."

Everyone stopped talking, and Elly's mouth formed a perfect "O" shape. The patter of the rain against the sidewalk was in concert with the Miles Davis song in the background.

"You mean like a vacation?" Barbara asked.

"Something like that," Stella said. "And not just up the road to Santa Barbara," she added. "Somewhere different." The headlights from a car making a U-turn momentarily lit up Stella's face. The others turned to look out the window and then back to Stella.

Almost as if she had planned it or was expecting this moment, Mary made what sounded more like a proclamation than a suggestion. "I propose Taos, New Mexico."

Stella laughed, and everyone's attention turned to Mary. Elly's mouth formed a second "O." They were silent and still, except for Mary stirring the spoon in her tea.

"And in winter," Mary confidently added.

It turned out that Mary had become enchanted with Taos and New Mexico after discovering the work of the writer and artist Natalie Goldberg through books she bought at the Wild Librarian.

She had mentioned Goldberg at times during club meetings, but no one could recall her thoughts on New Mexico. Mary began to share about the draw of the land for artists and other creative people. The discussion that ensued ended up going long into the evening after the other customers went on their way, and even after Grace put up the "closed" sign and locked the front door. They felt something good and magical was unfurling around them. They were caught up in the same spell.

Plans for the Taos trip commenced over the next several months, including during several gatherings in Stella's office where they ate dozens of muffins, cookies, and cupcakes while drinking coffee much too late, causing the women to often be awake in their beds well past midnight, feeling exhilarated while imagining their New Mexico trip. They also daydreamed about their journey. While baking or ringing up customers, Stella's mind was equally in the bakery and the vast desert landscape. Taos began to appear in Elly's poems even though the trip was months away. And Sheila and Barbara often talked about the trip over dinner. It wasn't that traveling was a big deal—some of them had even traveled quite extensively—but none of them had traveled together as a small group of women, and none of them had been to Taos.

Barbara searched online and found the perfect place for their adventure: a hotel and retreat center called the Mabel Dodge Luhan House. It turned out Mabel Dodge had been a major figure and cultivator of the arts in Taos. Her home, which was now a historic hotel that also held small workshops and retreats, featured guest rooms that had been rooms used by regular visitors, including Carl Jung, Georgia O'Keeffe, D. H. Lawrence, and Willa Cather. The women checked on availability and learned most of the rooms were available for the dates they were planning to stay. They discovered a solarium was available at a higher cost, providing expansive views of the landscape, including the Taos Sacred Mountain. Mary, caught up in the excitement, independently made a reservation for herself in the solarium and then informed the others several days later when they gathered to finalize their plans. Although this action was seen as a bit rude, Mary's excitement and the fact she had recommended New Mexico softened the others.

"Just know, Mary, that you are going to invite us up to your special room to hang out, and we won't take no for an answer," Stella said.

The others quickly made their reservations. Stella would be staying in what was called "Tony's Room," once the room of Mabel Dodge Luhan's husband; Barbara and Sheila reserved the "Ansel Adams Room;" and Elly went for Mabel Dodge Luhan's room, which was said to provide a view of the mesa and Sacred Mountain. "Ah," Mary said, "perfect for a poet." Barbara and Sheila were giddy over the fact Dennis Hopper had stayed in the room they'd reserved while he edited *Easy Rider*.

Over the next several months, the women continued to eat dozens of muffins, cookies, and cupcakes while drinking too much coffee. When they gathered at a table in the public area of the bakery bookstore, their laughter and excitement was contagious. Once, while they got carried away giggling and talking loudly about the famous people who had stayed at their upcoming destination, Nina Simone's song "Feeling Good" came on through the stereo system. Stella stood up and began to shake her hips, causing Grace to step out from behind the counter and join her in an impromptu dance. Soon, the whole group was up dancing, likely also a bit intoxicated from the caffeine and sugar. Other bakery customers watched this spontaneous display with large smiles.

An elderly man sitting near the window reading a book and enjoying a hot chocolate during his first visit thought, *What a curious place.* He put his mug and book down and started clapping in rhythm to the song. When things quieted down later and he eventually got up to leave, he called out to Stella from the door, "Great place! I'm definitely coming back!"

The Women Who Run With the Wolves Book Club members flew into Albuquerque on a cold Monday in January. It wasn't snowing when they landed, but snow was still on the ground. They waited outside for a shuttle to take them to the rental car area.

"Do you know why it's not snowing?" Stella asked as they tried to acclimate to the zero temperature. It was already seventy degrees when they left LAX in the morning. "It's not snowing," she exclaimed, "because it's too damn cold! I remember this from when I was a little girl growing up on the East Coast."

"Hurry!" Mary yelled when they saw the shuttle turning a corner in the distance and making its slow approach to them. When it stopped and the driver opened the door, Mary pushed ahead of everyone, including two men who were also waiting, and ran up the stairs to find a seat.

They laughed.

"Just like booking the solarium!" Elly told the others. "You know," she said, "Mary is an Aries. A fierce, independent ram. We need to keep this in mind."

They laughed more.

The women rented an SUV and began their drive to Taos with Elly at the wheel. The roads were plowed well. It had been days since it last snowed, so they had no issues making their way. The landscape was stark and breathtaking, with the snow covering the desert floor and the mountains surrounding them making it especially luminous.

When they arrived in Taos, it was dusk. Warm and inviting lights shone through many of the restaurant, gallery, and shop windows. They commented on the Pueblo architecture.

Finding the hotel the first time turned out to be tricky, requiring several loops around the center of town and resulting in near constant laughter until they turned the right way down a side street. The narrow street resembled an alley that turned into a bumpy gravel road. Elly slowed down, and they crept along until the hotel appeared. It looked exactly like the photos they had seen on the website.

"Oh my!" Sheila said for all of them.

Barbara and Sheila's room was part of a newer addition attached to the original historic home. Stella, Elly, and Mary were staying in the original structure. The three were delighted to discover their rooms were located up a steep wooden staircase that could only be reached by passing through the lodge's small bookstore. The woman working at the bookstore told them they were welcome to peruse the small collection after-hours since their rooms gave them twenty-four-hour access. Stella could not believe her good fortune to still have a bookstore so close even while she was away from the bakery.

They took their time reviewing the books, laughing and elbowing each other when they discovered several books by Estés and Goldberg on the shelves. There were books by and about earlier guests of the hotel, including D. H. Lawrence and Georgia O'Keeffe. The store even had several books on living a creative life. It was almost a mini version of the Wild Librarian.

Stella's room was closest to the bookstore, with Elly's down the hallway and Mary's solarium an additional steep climb to the highest level. Stella's room opened onto a large sleeping porch. Although it was too cold at the time to spend more than a few minutes sitting on the porch, she still ventured out each morning to take in the expansive view it provided. While in her room or on the porch, Stella could sometimes hear Mary walking around on the hardwood floors of the solarium above or Elly walking down the hallway just outside her door. It was the most intimate the women had been with each other, as if they were temporarily sharing a house. During the stay, Stella fell asleep peacefully each night, feeling the calming energy of the books beneath her and her women friends above and close by.

The first morning, they met in the old wood-paneled dining room to discover an amazing breakfast buffet. Stella was pleased to have numerous vegan options to choose from. She made herself a large bowl of oatmeal topped with berries, brown sugar, and almond milk. Elly sat next to her in one of the room's handsomely carved wood chairs. Her chair creaked as she leaned over toward Stella to share a discovery in a dramatic whisper: "The floor in my room is painted turquoise!"

"Mine too!" Stella replied. She told Elly about the tiles she discovered in her bathroom, which were hand-painted by D. H.

Lawrence in the 1920s.

"No way!" Elly's eyes widened, and her mouth formed its "O" shape.

Mary, Sheila, and Barbara appeared at the same time to join them. Mary ate a large slice of a breakfast bread with nuts, letting out a moan as she chewed.

"Mary," Stella said, "you're almost being inappropriate with those sounds."

After finishing the bread, Mary got up for seconds and brought an even larger slice to the table. "Oh, Stella!" she said. "You must find out how to make a vegan version of this for the Wild Librarian. I'll be eternally grateful."

"I'll see what I can do," Stella said with a wink. "Sheila and Barbara!" she continued. "Guess what? Mary, Elly, and I discovered after checking in that our rooms are above a small bookstore."

"That's amazing," Sheila said.

"Yes, and can you believe they have some of Dr. E's books in there?"

"No! Oh, this is the perfect place for us." Sheila beamed.

"Cheers!" Mary called out, raising her orange juice. They clinked their juice glasses and coffee mugs together.

"Cheers to the Wild Librarian for making this all possible! Cheers to Stella!" Elly declared.

They remained for a long time in the dining room while other guests finished eating and left to get on with their days. Without discussing it, all five of them felt a desire to go slow.

When they finally made their way outside, it was late morning. They spent their first day walking around town, visiting art galleries and shops. Stella took a detour to visit the Taos Public Library while the others waited nearby at a small café. Feeling tired from the walking and travel the day before, they ate an early dinner and decided to join Mary in the solarium. First, they all stopped at Stella's bathroom so she could show them the D. H. Lawrence tiles. Everyone wanted to touch the ceramic work and take photos.

"I never knew a bathroom could be so romantic," Elly said as her fingers played with the white fabric shower curtain that circled a large freestanding vintage bathtub.

After the bathroom explorations, they took a peek at the sleeping porch off Stella's room before ascending to Mary's. The walk up the steep and narrow solarium steps was not comfortable for everyone. Barbara commented she wasn't sure she would be visiting the steep room again, but once they were there, it was worth it. Just as the website said, the room featured wraparound glass windows. Being dark, it was mysterious and even a bit spooky until they got used to the vast darkness beyond them. They assembled themselves on Mary's bed and two side chairs. When they moved, the wood floors creaked in response.

"This is really something," Elly said. "Look at all the stars."

"It's strange," Mary said, "but sometimes when I experience something so unique and special like this, I think of Don. It's been many long years, but I imagine him and wonder if he can see me. Does he know what I'm up to and that I'm sitting in this extraordinary place?"

Everyone recognized Don as Mary's deceased husband whom she spoke of infrequently, but always with an intensity when she did. Don had been a new architect with much promise when he passed in the car accident.

"What would he say, Mary?" Stella asked. "If he could see you right now, what do you think he would say?"

Mary ran her hand over the soft blankets on her bed. "I know exactly what he would say," she told Stella and the others. "He would say, 'Go for it, Mary. You go for it.' He lived life like that—with gusto."

"Ah!" Elly said. "He sounds like he was such a wonderful man."

The small gathering in the solarium continued until the women were too tired to talk and they retreated to their rooms for a deep sleep. The next morning, they rose early and made their way out to Abiquiu to take a landscape tour near Georgia O'Keefe's Ghost Ranch house. While driving there, the women discovered Mary had what appeared to be half the morning's nut bread loaf on her lap. They laughed while she ate away with a blissful look on her face. Seeing this, Stella thought of Don and his "gusto" and considered how joyful their marriage must have been.

"Aries the Ram, Mary!" Elly cheered. "The first fire sign of the Zodiac!" They laughed more, and Mary gave a thumbs-up.

When they reached Abiquiu, they discovered the tour would take place in a rickety shuttle bus. Along with several other guests, they climbed in and got seats near each other. A young man was listening to music they could hear faintly through his headphones. Stella recognized the song "Ventura Highway" and hummed along to the line, "The free wind is blowing through your hair . . ." The bus stopped at different spots, and everyone got out to take in the landscape. The tour guide held up images of O'Keefe's paintings to show the similarities with various landmarks. It revealed how slowly time moved out there.

Near the Ghost Ranch, everyone got out again and looked at O'Keefe's house in the distance. It was undergoing restoration and was not accessible. The guide pointed toward the roof and commented on how O'Keefe had liked to sleep up there, an area she accessed via a ladder.

"Where is the kitchen?" Stella asked, and the guide pointed again. Stella viewed photographs of O'Keefe's kitchen in the past, so even though she could not see it at this moment she could imagine what had been inside. She felt a pull toward the bakery and her magical industrial oven. She wondered how things were going there. It was Wednesday, so they would be serving several dozen On the Road Chocolate Cupcakes for the open mic in the evening. Stella smiled to herself thinking of the Wild Librarian—steady, successful, and awaiting her return.

Later that night, when they returned to Taos from Abiquiu, the women ate at a bar and grill called the Gorge in the center of town. They made the short walk to the restaurant from the lodge. Barbara commented on the moon and stars, and they all looked up. As they got close to the Gorge, they could hear live music. A rock band was set up in the parking lot of a small cafe. They stood with a small crowd when an accordion player from the band moved forward prominently to play a solo, the beautiful notes filling the air before the drummer accompanied him. It was unusual to see an accordion player in a band like this. Stella's heart soared as she thought of Guy Mandal, the shy musician who sometimes stopped in for coffee before playing his accordion at a park in Santa Ana. Since his arrival shortly after the bakery first opened, Stella and Andy had hired him several times for events, which had led to him being occasionally hired throughout the city.

After a few songs, the women continued to the restaurant. Over dinner, they decided to spend the next day—their last day before returning home—visiting galleries and walking around town. Without needing to say it, they all knew their experiment in traveling together had been a wonderful success.

While waiting to board their flight from Albuquerque back to Santa Ana, Mary suddenly placed herself in the middle of them all and said, "I propose we go to Montana next." Taken by surprise, since the statement had come out of context, no one immediately responded. Mary then added, "In late spring."

Mary shared she had already conducted some research on her phone while they were at the lodge. She'd kept the information to herself like a delicious, perfect gift to be presented at the right moment. On the flight home, they began their first reminisces of Taos while playing with the idea of Montana.

Back at the Wild Librarian, Stella saw things were in good order. The time away had been her longest since the bakery opened. She picked Jane up from her neighbor and found her to be her usual robust and happy self. She tightly hugged her while she let out several of her signature howls and snorts.

It would be wrong to say that everything returned to normal after coming home, although some things definitely did, such as the day-to-day running of the bakery. But the trip to Taos—the magic, serenity, and comradery of it—stayed with Stella. Her previous work at the college provided a sense of community, but it had been years—almost three decades, if she had to guess—since she'd felt the deep sense of belonging the small group offered. She realized how much the bakery had given her and wished her parents were here to see her life now, at this moment. "Thank you," she said out loud, nodding and placing her hands together near her chest.

At the next gathering of the book club, no other members showed except for the core group, so they went to Stella's office. Once they were gathered, Stella stepped out and returned holding a turquoise plate. She placed it on her desk where they could all see what she had created.

"Is that what I think it is?" Mary asked.

"Indeed," Stella told her. "Taos Bread!"

Before leaving Taos, Stella had been able to secure the recipe from the lodge's chef. It was a simple bread of pumpkin, pecans, and walnuts with just enough cinnamon, vanilla, and ginger. Stella made muffins instead of a loaf, sprinkled the tops with a little raw sugar and pecan shavings before baking, and used applesauce as an egg replacer.

She handed each woman a muffin, but they all waited for Mary to take the first bite and report back. She chewed, closed her eyes, opened her eyes but said nothing, took another bite, closed her eyes, chewed, and then made one of her inappropriate moans.

"We have our answer!" Barbara declared, and they all dug in.

"This is truly divine, Stella," Mary said. "I think we have started a tradition tonight. Taos Bread for future meetings!"

They started by reading a few pages on creativity from *Women Who Run With the Wolves* and shared their thoughts. As things began to wind down, they continued their discussion from the plane about the possibility of a Montana trip. Mary had located a bed-and-breakfast at a wolf sanctuary outside Bozeman called the Moon Inn. It featured a log cabin-style house with a wraparound porch adjacent to where the wolves lived. They looked the place up on Stella's computer. The women read about how wolves were brought there to live out their lives after being captive in zoos or following a period of rehabilitation after sustaining injuries in the wild. Before long, they booked their stay, and the next adventure was upon them in a few short months.

The women arrived in Montana in late May. On their drive from the Bozeman airport to the sanctuary they stopped at a co-op grocery store for lunch. The co-op had a large casual dining area with a salad bar and hot bar. While dipping the crust of her cornbread into the store's vegan chili, Stella glanced at Mary sitting across from her and noticed she looked sleepy. Her movements as she ate were sluggish.

"Are you tired, Mary?" Stella asked her.

Mary quickly looked up with a surprised expression. "Oh, just a bit. I suppose from the early flight."

"Boy, I know I could use a nap," Elly said, joining them with a salad in one hand and a large coffee in the other.

They mostly ate in silence, anticipating their arrival at the sanctuary. Outside the tall windows of the co-op eating area were magnificent wispy trees with long, thin branches. When the wind blew, they made a barely audible scratching sound on the glass.

Before leaving, they walked around the store together filling a small shopping cart with various goodies to have in their cabin rooms or keep in the shared refrigerator they'd read about. They bought gourmet olive oil popcorn, chocolate bars, cookies, chips, pretzels, a few instant soups, coconut milk creamer for Stella's morning coffee, and yogurt. Elly tossed a locally made rose bubble bath concoction into the basket. "Just in case," she said, winking at the others. They laughed and tossed in a few more bottles.

Driving through Bozeman on their way to the Moon Inn, they pointed out places to look at over the next few days: coffeehouses, a dive bar called the Velvet Hour, and a small bookstore that made

Stella scream while clapping her hands. When they reached the Moon Inn, it was just early evening. There would still be several hours of light.

They ciscovered the wolves were adjacent to the cabin within two large enclosures that contained grass and numerous trees and bushes. Only a tall chain-link fence running the perimeter of the enclosures separated the wolves from the rest of the land.

"There are the two packs," Sheila said. Within one of the enclosures, the women saw three wolves, and the other contained five, including a large majestic white wolf.

"Wow!" Stella's toes moved within her boots.

As they approached the wolves, they noticed signs warning them not to touch the fence or the animals. They got up close to the enclosure where the pack of five lived.

"It's like us," Barbara said, pointing. "See? Five."

This made everyone smile, and a good, warm feeling fell around them.

"Hello!" they heard a woman's voice calling. She was walking down the cabin stairs toward them. The woman looked like a Montana version of Stella wearing jeans, work boots, and an oversize flannel shirt over a T-shirt. "You must be the Stella Peabody group," she said, taking them all in, "or, as I understand it, The Women Who Run With the Wolves."

Stella extended her hand, laughing. "Yes, that's us. I'm Stella."

The woman introduced herself as Sandy and asked them if they had eaten yet. They told her about heading to the co-op from the airport.

"We always do food research before," Barbara told Sandy. "Stella is a vegan and a former librarian, so the combo works in our benefit."

Sandy went into telling them about the policies and when breakfast was served in the mornings. The women half-listened out of politeness, their attention drawn to the wolves, who were now making their way close to them on the other side of the fence. The large white one made a raspy sound as he deliberately and gracefully moved his legs along, in front of the others. Stella and Mary instinctively moved a few inches closer to the fence.

"That's Commander," Sandy told them, nodding toward the white wolf.

"He's stunning," Barbara said. "Look at his coat. My, my."

"He's currently the alpha male or leader of the pack," they heard Sandy say, but her voice seemed faraway as they took in the large body of the magnificent wolf. The other wolves were close in size to large German shepherd dogs, but Commander had several more inches of height and girth on him. The women could hear their paws in the tall grass as they got within a few feet. They stood, the five wolves and the five women, investigating each other. This lasted for a few minutes.

A light wind kicked up, coming through the tall grass, rippling softly through the women's hair and the wolves' fur, until it landed and came to a rest within some bushes. Commander then surprised them by coming over and rubbing his body against the fence right in front of them.

"Look," Mary said, pointing toward the ground. Pooled in clumps along the fence were groupings of white and gray fur.

"They are still shedding," Sandy explained, making them aware of her existence again and pulling them halfway out of the spell. "Ladies," she said, "make sure you always keep a little distance." She explained how she went into the enclosure daily with a hired man to feed them, but they wore heavy protective gear that covered everything from their feet to the tops of their heads.

"You will see," Sandy said, "that they jump on us and play like friendly dogs. They are used to people, but you must remember they are wolves, not dogs."

Commander kept rubbing his side against the fence.

"He has a scratch, or he wants us to pet him," Sheila said.

All of a sudden, Stella started giggling until her giggles turned into uncontrollable, giddy laughter. Elly joined her. Their laughter became louder and more joyous. It was a celebration brought on by the exhilaration of the wolves coupled with their weariness from all the travel. Soon, they were all laughing while Commander and the rest of the pack watched them. Then Commander backed up a bit, tilted his head, and let out a howl. Stella thought of Jane. It was a full-bodied sound that made them first hush, but then become giddy again. As they laughed, the rest of the pack joined in with howls, each one carrying a unique tone and vibration. An old female wolf Sandy pointed out made a screechy sound as she bellowed with her thin muzzle in the air.

This greeting went on for a good ten minutes. Stella wiped tears from her eyes. After one of the wolves let out a final little grunt, it grew quiet. They stood in amazement, looking at each other. Stella noticed Sandy was no longer there. In the distance, they could hear a car approaching on the highway. It came closer until it passed by them, made the bend in the road, and continued on. The car sounds gently brought them back from where they had been transported.

"This is definitely a once-in-a-lifetime thing," Mary said. There was a firm tone to her voice as if something important had been spoken. She closed her eyes and brought her hands together in a prayer in front of her.

Elly came to Mary's side and put an arm around her shoulders.

"Well," Mary told them, "I think that flight did knock the wind out of me. Let's go find out about our rooms."

The next morning, Stella found herself alone for a few minutes in the communal dining room at the cabin. The sun was just coming up. She saw coffee had already been prepared, so she poured a large cup and walked over to look out the window above the kitchen sink. The small wolf pack was resting in the grass. The larger pack, including Commander, was milling about. Stella saw a figure appear—Mary. She watched as Commander came over and pushed up against the fence as he did the day before. Stella was startled to see Mary reach out and touch the fence too. Commander rubbed his body around like a cat.

Stella wondered if Mary was touching him. She left the cabin and started walking toward her. As she approached, Commander was still pressed against the fence, but Mary was bent far over at the waist and putting her hands near the ground.

"Mary," Stella said quietly.

Mary stood, and Stella noticed her hands were full of white fur. "Look how magical," she said.

"Were you touching him?" Stella asked.

"Yes," Mary told her. She put the fur inside the pockets of her blue coat, some of it peeking out like stuffing.

Stella looked at Commander's large body pushed against the fence. She looked into his large brown eyes. "You try too," he seemed to say. Her heart was racing. She looked at Commander's eyes again and started to raise her hand. She paused, weighing the danger.

"Go for it," Mary said.

Stella decided she could put her hand flat against the fence and easily pull back if the wolf made a sudden movement. She pressed her right hand against the fence, feeling Commander's fur and the amazing strength and firmness of his side. Mary put her hand up again, and they both stood there feeling his fur. The other wolves stayed a few feet away, watching.

Commander kept his eyes on Mary and Stella. It was quiet, and the women felt lost and dreamy, dipped in a pocket outside of time.

Mary put her hand over Stella's. "You have become a good friend, Stella," Mary told her, looking serious, yet with a small smile. Stella noticed Mary's eyes had teared up.

"I feel the same about you, Mary," Stella said.

There was something about Mary's voice though, that firm tone again, and the seriousness of her face that stirred up a concern in Stella.

While in Montana, Mary enjoyed the wolves and did her best to hide her anxiety from the others. She was not anticipating a creeping tired feeling would begin and turn into dips of exhaustion, causing her to back out of a few outings.

"Is everything okay, Mary?" Elly asked when she told them she was going to skip a hike around the sanctuary grounds for a second time.

"I may be coming down with a cold," Mary responded.

"Rest well," Stella told her, "and we'll come get you in time for lunch. We're going to the co-op in town again."

"And that great little bookstore!" Sheila added.

Oh boy, Mary thought, and she felt even more tired. The winding country road. The possibility of them getting lost again on the way back. She was the one who had planned this trip with such enthusiasm, and now she wanted to mostly rest, visit with the wolves each day, and make her way back to California, where she believed she would feel safer. She walked from the covered porch where the women were gathered to the interior stairs of the cabin until she reached her bed and fell instantly asleep.

The others didn't know that before leaving for Montana Mary had been for a biopsy. Her left breast. It had all happened suddenly and unexpectedly within a few weeks of her annual mammogram. The day after, she'd felt sluggish and some pain at the incision, but then she bounced back. She kept a full schedule at her office, seeing ongoing clients and a few new ones, including a middle-aged married couple. The husband began the appointment with an announcement: "We're here to get help in coping with my wife's cancer." Mary's heart pounded at the word. Was it a sign? She told herself not to be foolish and moved on with the week. She dipped into the Wild Librarian a few times for coffee and a quick chat with Stella.

Then the Montana trip was upon Mary and the other women. She was to see her doctor two days after their return to California. *Why ruin everyone's fun?* she thought. Besides, she sometimes felt like her regular self—until the moment they were waiting for their connecting flight to Bozeman. Suddenly, a slow nervousness started about being so far from home. It would last the four days of their excursion. Even when she was amid joy, an ominous feeling hung overhead. She felt the most peaceful in the presence of Commander and the other wolves.

Mary considered telling the others one night when they were sitting around the large table in the cabin's shared dining room. The women had spontaneously gone out to an open mic they'd heard about that afternoon on the local public radio station. Mary felt up to it, so she went along this time. She drank a little wine with the others, and they all cheered for Elly when she got up to read a few short poems. Now, they were at the cabin reminiscing about the night and making comments on the other poets. This was their last night before returning home to California.

The desire to share her news with the others, including wanting them to know her left breast was feeling sore, started to tear at Mary. Here she was facing a difficult unknown, and for once, she had a group of kind and supportive women friends, yet Mary's decades of privacy won over her desire to share something she found both scary and deeply personal. She retreated into herself and kept her fear and secret bottled up.

The book club's flight from Montana landed at LAX. Sheila and Barbara made their way to Santa Monica while Mary and Elly piled into Stella's Subaru on their way to Elly's in Long Beach and then to Santa Ana. Mary had left her car at Stella's. Mary got in the back, noticing a clump of Jane's fur on the seat. She didn't even take the time to move it but fell into the seat, feeling a rush of relief. She would soon be home.

It was Monday evening. Her doctor's appointment was on Wednesday morning. *I have a whole day to prepare*, she told herself and closed her eyes as Stella made her way onto the 405. Mary opened her travel bag on the seat next to her and reached inside, feeling the small container she knew held Commander's fur.

Mary slept in the next morning with her cat, Dr. Freud, curled up against the small of her back. She made coffee and went out to sit under her avocado tree. Instead of reading the newspaper or a few pages from a book as she usually did, she sat with her bare feet in the grass picking yellow paint off a corner of the chair and looking toward the house. Dr. Freud was sitting by the French doors watching her. She looked at the Mexican tiles in the garden path until she found her favorite one of the crescent moon. She got up and knelt on the ground, placing her hand flat on it.

The tile was already warming up from the morning sun. Mary looked at her hand. It seemed weathered, old. Had it looked like that for a while? *What else about my body has changed?* she wondered. She returned to her writing desk inside and mostly organized papers and looked over some brochures she'd brought home from the trip.

The day was quiet and still; it seemed to effortlessly slip away. Before bed, Mary prepared a relaxing bath while listening to her favorite college jazz station. While in the bath, she placed her right hand on her left breast and closed her eyes. She started to softly cry.

While Mary cried in her bathtub, the other women, unaware of what she was carrying, went about their evenings in their usual tempos with the magic of the wolves still encircling them. Sheila and Barbara had two of their grandchildren over. They were engaged in multiple games of Clue. Elly was sitting at her computer editing another writer's novel—work she did to financially support her own life as a poet. And Stella was home from the bakery, curled up in bed reading with Jane snoring away next to her.

In the morning, Stella would be picking up a shipment from Riviera's Spice Shop. She was excited to begin experimenting with new recipes inspired by the Montana adventure. Stella imagined Commander and the pack were likely asleep with their bodies resting in the tall grass.

Of course, none of them knew what would soon be upon them and what Mary would have to endure.

Coconut Jazz Muffins
Recipe for approximately 18 muffins

2 cups unbleached organic flour

1/2 cup organic shredded coconut

1 cup organic raw sugar

1/3 cup unsweetened applesauce

1 teaspoon baking powder

1 can (14 ounces) organic coconut milk*

1 teaspoon baking soda

1 teaspoon organic vanilla extract

1/2 teaspoon salt

Preheat oven to 350 degrees. Mix together the flour, sugar, baking powder, baking soda, and salt. Separately, blend the coconut milk, applesauce, and vanilla. Add the wet mixture to the dry mixture until combined well, but do not overmix. Add the shredded coconut. Pour the batter into your baking cups. To make these extra good, sprinkle a little coconut on top before baking! Bake for 18–22 minutes. To make sure the muffins are ready, insert a toothpick near the center of one. If the toothpick comes out clean, you know they are done! If any batter sticks to the toothpick, they need to bake for longer.

*Coconut milk that comes in cans is highly recommended for this recipe. This is usually found in the Asian food section of the grocery store.

PERFECT PAIRING: Ah! Any Toni Morrison will do as your taste buds revel in each sweet and heavenly bite.

Wild Women Blueberry Muffins
Recipe for 12 muffins

1 1/2 cups unbleached organic flour
3/4 cup organic almond milk
1/2 cup organic raw sugar
1/4 cup organic oil
2 teaspoons baking powder
3/4 cup frozen organic wild
1 teaspoon salt
blueberries
a little extra organic raw sugar

Preheat oven to 400 degrees. Mix dry ingredients together first. Add almond milk and oil. Fold in the blueberries. Batter will be lumpy. Fun! Use a spoon to put batter into your baking cups. Sprinkle a little of the extra raw sugar on top before putting them in the oven. Bake for 18–24 minutes. To make sure the muffins are ready, insert a toothpick near the center of one. If the toothpick comes out clean, you know they are done! If any batter sticks to the toothpick, they need to bake for longer.

Other Possibilities: This recipe calls out for experimentation! Possibilities include adding a bit of cinnamon, walnuts, pecans, and even shredded coconut. Go wild and free!

PERFECT PAIRING: Of course, the book *Women Who Run With the Wolves* is recommended to accompany this delicious treat! Stella also recommends listing to Estés' wonderful *Theatre of the Imagination* to be swept away by folktales and poetry. Indulge, howl, and unleash your wild spirit.

Dr. Freud, an Avocado Tree, and the Goddess Spaceship

Mary Chin's solitary life began after her husband Don's sudden death when they were in their early thirties. She now owned the house they'd rented as young professionals getting their footing. After nearly three decades, it had undergone some renovation, yet what Mary considered the "soul" remained the same: the original wood floors, the built-in cabinets, and most of the bright Mexican tiles Don added to the back porch and walkway in the garden. At the time of his passing, they were beginning to experience the great promise Don's work as an architect would bring them. An old avocado tree they planted together had continued to flourish over the years. Mary would sit beneath its canopy reading most mornings throughout the year on a large wooden chair she'd painted bright yellow.

Like some other therapists Mary knew, she was great at advising others on grief and how to "move on" and "start over," but she didn't want to do either within the context of her own life. She felt she had experienced a great romance. So great, in fact, she had no desire for another. "It was enough for three lifetimes," she once told Stella while having coffee in her office at the Wild Librarian.

Instead of romance, Mary devoted herself to her work with a great passion. Beyond her thriving private practice, she attended conferences, presented papers, and found happiness through being what she considered a lifelong student. When she came across a notice about the Women Who Run With the Wolves Book Club, she was thrilled to meet up with others interested in the work of Estés, but she didn't imagine anything more. She certainly didn't anticipate the circle of friends she would soon have and her openness to Stella and the others. Still, when she was at a time of need, feeling ill and concerned about the pending results of her left breast biopsy, retreating to her private refuge was her impulse. It made her feel safe. *I need to figure this out first*, she told herself, although she wasn't sure what "this" meant.

For the monthly book club meeting following the core members' trip to Montana, two new younger women came to participate. The topic was on the archetype of the crone and elder wisdom. Stella tried a new recipe of spice cake with a cinnamon crumble topping. It was rich, layered, and paired perfectly with the discussion. Mary never showed. After the meeting, Stella and the core members went back to her office to hang out for a bit. None of them had received a text from Mary, but Stella checked her email and found Mary wrote to her earlier in the day about traveling to New York for a conference and needing to miss the meeting. No one thought much of it.

The following month, three women who said they'd heard about the group "through the grapevine" joined them. This time, Stella asked them to be the taste testers of a hearty sweet potato bread from a new recipe. It had fresh spices she'd picked up earlier in the week from Riviera's Spice Shop next door. It was quickly devoured.

"What will this one be?" Elly asked.

"In college, I fell in love with Judy Grahn's *Common Women Poems*. Are any of you familiar with her?" No one was. "Oh!" Stella went on. "I'll have to find my old copy and share it with you all. The ingredients of this bread—so common and simple, yet hearty and exquisite, remind me of Judy's poems."

"So," Sheila asked, "Judy's Bread?"

"I like that. Yes, Judy's Bread!" Stella decided, picking up her coffee mug in a salute.

With full and content bellies, they discussed the complicated figure of Baba Yaga from Slavic folklore that was present in Estés' work. Mary had written to Stella and the others earlier in the week to say she was battling the flu and would likely not make it. Barbara said she'd reached out to her. "She sounded terrible," she told the others. "We only talked for a moment. She said she had medicine and didn't need anything."

Then it happened again. Mary sent an email before the next monthly meeting explaining she was making a presentation in Boston for a psychology retreat and would be traveling all week. "Missing you all very much," she wrote. "Looking forward to seeing you next time." The group had an unusual and exciting surprise guest, a folklorist from UCLA, so they got caught up in the reverie and didn't think much about Mary not being able to attend until they were cleaning up and Elly said, "I sure miss Mary being here. She would have loved tonight. I miss our fierce Aries ram!" They laughed and agreed.

"I'm going to check in with her in a few days when she's back from Boston," Stella said.

Stella was alone with Grace early the next morning when the first clue arrived indicating something was wrong.

"I haven't seen Mary around here lately," Grace said. "Is she okay?" Grace was stocking cups and napkins near the bakery case while Stella was arranging copies of Kerouac's novel *On the Road* to accompany the On the Road Chocolate Cupcakes she'd just baked. Several dozen cupcakes were already arranged in their neat rows in the bakery case, with half sprinkled with powdered sugar, and the other half with chocolate frosting.

"Mary was ill and has been traveling," Stella told Grace. "She had two conferences recently. She's on the East Coast this week."

"That's odd," Grace said, "'cause I could swear I saw her yesterday."

"Really?" Stella said, stopping her work to look at Grace. She put her hands inside the front pockets of her apron. "Where?"

"At the medical plaza across from St. Jude in Fullerton." Grace stacked the last of the cups and walked over to check the cash register. "It was the oddest thing."

"What was?" Stella asked, starting to feel unsettled. She took one of her hands out of the apron pocket and ran it over the soft, cool cover of a book while looking intently at Grace.

"Well . . ." Grace opened the cash drawer, causing it to make its customary metal clang. Although she must have heard the sound thousands of times, it startled Stella, and she noticed how it vibrated and hung in the air. "I was in the lobby near the parking garage when I saw Mary come out of the elevator. Her posture was different, like she was hunched over. I was only about ten feet away. I swear it was her. She was carrying that large red purse she bought when you guys went to New Mexico."

"What happened?" Stella asked.

A noise near the entrance made them both turn to look toward the street, where a few customers were already waiting to come in.

"We still have a few minutes," Stella said. "Tell me."

"Well, nothing really happened. That's what I mean—it was odd. I called out to her twice. I don't know how she couldn't have heard me. No one else was around. But she ignored me and kept on going."

"That doesn't sound like Mary," Stella said. "She never misses an opportunity to say hello."

"I know. It was strange, but once I came back here, I got busy and forgot about it until I saw she wasn't at your book club again."

"And you're sure it was Mary?"

"Ninety-nine percent sure," Grace said, adjusting the black metal bobby pins that held her bun in place and starting to walk toward the door to let the first customers in.

As soon as she could get away from helping Grace with the morning rush, Stella went into her office and called Mary. She reached her voice mail and left a message for her to call back when she could. Then she called Elly. As they talked about what Grace told Stella, their concern grew until Stella said she would try Mary one more time later in the morning. Elly said she would send a text and let Stella know if she heard anything. By early afternoon, they'd received no response, so Stella decided to go to Mary's office.

Mary's office was on the second floor of one of the city's many old, charming office buildings. Stella had never been, but she dug around in her wallet and found the address of Mary's practice on her business card. When she reached the door, the unsettled feeling she'd had all morning grew when she noticed two missed delivery slips stuck to the door frame. Stella checked the dates, noticing they were from the week before. The door had a mail slot. Vertical blinds in a window near the door were slightly open, so Stella was able to peer inside and see a part of the carpeted floor. At least several dozen envelopes, some flyers, and a few magazines that had been put through the mail slot spilled out in a disarray on the carpet.

Stella was starting to leave when a man came out of the adjacent office. "Excuse me," she said.

The man continued locking his door.

"Excuse me," Stella said, louder.

"Yes?"

"Have you seen Mary around?"

"Are you one of her patients?" he asked.

"No, I'm her friend."

"I see," he said. "I can't really say. I'm in and out like her with appointments. I'd say it's been a few weeks maybe since I've seen her." He shrugged and walked away while Stella's stomach churned.

She drove her car near the Washington Square neighborhood located a few short miles from the Wild Librarian. She had only seen where Mary lived once before, and it had been about a year ago in the dark when she gave her a ride home from a mechanic's garage. Was it Lowell? Or maybe Baker? Stella dipped into her memory, trying to recall the right street. She drove down Lowell first, slowly and twice in both directions. Nothing rang a bell. She made her way to Baker.

After turning, she saw an elementary school. This gave her memory a jolt. She slowed down more, remembering Mary's house was located across from the school. She rolled down her window, hearing the children. The small street was congested with cars and a school bus. It was still the afternoon and school was getting out.

Stella found parking on the next street over. She made her way back to examine the houses across from the school. The afternoon sun was hot. She pulled off her jacket and tied it around her waist. Directly across from the playground, she spotted a small Spanish bungalow. The turquoise trim around a large picture window made Stella stop. It was the same color as the floors at the Mabel Dodge Luhan House in Taos where the book club had stayed during their trip. Stella remembered Mary telling them about painting the trim, feeling inspired by the New Mexico adventure. This had to be her house.

She walked up the sidewalk and saw a tuxedo cat sunbathing in the window. Seeing Stella, the cat stood, arched its back, yawned, and returned to its lazy reclining pose. "I know who you are," Stella said out loud. Although she had only seen photos, she knew the cat must be Mary's beloved Dr. Freud. His ease and shiny coat gave Stella a hopeful feeling that everything must be okay. She wondered if she was overreacting. Maybe Grace was wrong.

Everything was quiet, but then the sounds of children still lingering at the school came back into Stella's awareness. "I told you yesterday," she heard a girl's impatient voice say in the distance. Someone started bouncing a ball. Stella walked up to Mary's door, noticing no mail or newspapers waiting to be retrieved. This was also a good sign. She knocked. There was no answer. Dr. Freud remained stationary in the window. Stella leaned in closer to the door to listen for any sounds.

A large tree and several bushes in the front yard cast a shadow over the door and created a slight buffer from some of the street noise. Someone was still bouncing a ball. Stella heard what sounded like a chain-link fence closing in the schoolyard. She knocked again. Dr. Freud got up and moved around but only returned to the same position.

Stella walked to the side of the house and made her way down the driveway. It was in the old style known as a Hollywood driveway with a strip of grass down the center of the concrete. Stella noticed the grass was well-manicured, giving no indication of neglect. There was a wood gate blocking access to the back yard, but she could see the roof of a detached garage at least two car lengths in the distance from where the house ended. She looked through an opening between the wood slats and saw the garage door was closed.

From what she could see, everything looked in order. Could Mary simply be in Boston and someone was picking up her mail and checking in on her cat? Could the mail at her office just be from one week and the man was wrong about Mary not being there for a long time? He did say he was in and out . . .

Stella decided to walk back and try the door once more. As she made her way, she looked over at the large picture window expecting to see Dr. Freud continuing with his sunbathing. She was startled to see Mary standing there holding Dr. Freud in her arms. She was wearing a long blue terry cloth robe. Their eyes met. Stella gathered herself from the surprise and made a small gesture with her hand that was more a sign of peace than a wave. She became aware she may be needlessly intruding on Mary by showing up like this, but as she looked, she could tell something was wrong. She saw the hunching Grace had described. Mary's eyes looked tired. Dr. Freud jumped down, and Mary moved her hand, pointing toward the door. Stella walked over.

When the door opened, Stella could see Mary's face better. She had dark circles and small bags under her eyes. Stella noticed a few small stains, possibly from coffee, on the front of Mary's robe. She was wearing gray socks that covered her calves where the robe ended, and she leaned against the doorframe looking at Stella. A hint of incense came from inside the house.

"Mary," Stella started, "I hope I'm not bothering you. We have been worried."

Mary didn't respond. Did she start to look a little sad? Stella couldn't be sure.

"Grace mentioned seeing you yesterday," Stella continued, feeling more uncomfortable. "We thought you were traveling, so I got concerned." She shifted her feet and noticed it was quiet on the street. The children must have all been picked up by now.

A few sticky purple blossoms from the jacaranda trees lining the street were bunched near the threshold to Mary's house as if they had blown there and got trapped with nowhere else to travel. Their purple vibrancy was faded yet still beautiful.

"Is everything okay?" Stella asked when Mary continued to remain silent.

"Stella," Mary began, "I'm sorry for my absence lately. I'm dealing with some issues and would like you to please respect my privacy." Although the words were delivered quietly, they carried a sharpness and finality she had never heard in Mary's voice. Elly's characterization of Mary as the Aries ram they all loved, charging forward first with independence, had changed into what sounded like a "back off" warning. The unsettled feeling kicked up in Stella's stomach, and her throat felt dry.

"Again, I'm sorry, Stella."

Before she could respond, Mary closed the door. Stella heard the latch of a deadbolt.

She stepped back and to the side so she could see the picture window. Dr. Freud was back to his sunbathing. Mary appeared and slowly pulled her white curtains closed. Stella watched how her movements had none of her usual agility. Mary never looked back at Stella. It was clear the encounter was over.

When Stella brought the news back to Grace and then relayed what had happened through a conference call with the women from the book club, everyone's concern heightened. There was speculation she may have suffered a nervous breakdown. Stella described the stained robe and the slowness of Mary's movements, yet she also shared about the well-maintained grass and no indication of neglect outside the house.

"Well, that's easy," Sheila said. "I'm sure she has a regular gardener, and it doesn't take much to open the door and grab your mail."

"I wish there was someone else we could ask—so that we wouldn't bother Mary," Elly said.

"I thought the same thing," Stella added, "but her immediate family is gone, and she has never mentioned any other relatives."

"Right," Barbara said. "I got the sense colleagues she knew through professional associations and all of us were her main relationships."

Elly offered a suggestion. "It's Wednesday. Let's sit on this until Friday. Stella sensed something was wrong, but it didn't sound like immediate danger. We know that at least the exterior of her home is in good order. If none of us hear from Mary tomorrow, let's consider going to her home on Friday."

Stella commented that she wasn't sure about waiting. She rolled the electrical cord for her desk lamp between her thumb and forefingers.

"Well," Elly said, "if you get nervous, Stella, you can always go back. Maybe take Grace or Andy with you next time, but what are you going to do if she just shuts you out again? Call the police?"

"That's true, Stella," Sheila chimed in. "Mary must know we've all heard about you going over there by now. Let's wait. Give her a day, and then we'll go. All of us together."

Stella couldn't sleep well. She kept picturing Mary's face and the stained robe. Stella's restlessness even bothered her dog, Jane. She jumped down from her usual spot at the foot of the bed and retreated to the guest room across the hall.

Images of Dr. Freud in the window floated around in Stella's exhausted mind until it was time to go into the Wild Librarian to get the day started.

"You look like hell," Andy said to Stella when she arrived. He was arranging the baked goods in the bakery case.

"Thanks, Andy. That's how I feel," Stella told him. She had only washed her face and pulled her unruly hair back with a rubber band.

She put her apron on and let out a sigh, tapping one of her boots on the floor.

"Andy, can you start a pot of coffee for me? I think I need the whole thing."

"Is it Mary?" he asked.

Stella looked at him with surprise.

"Grace was telling me about it," he said.

She brought Andy up to speed with some of the details while yawning and sighing.

"Stella, why don't you get out of here? Go home. I can handle the opening today," he offered, but Stella stayed.

"What would I do at home with this agitation I have?" she asked.

She got to work baking the Enchanted Lemon Pecan Cupcakes for the day. Andy brought her a piping-hot mug of coffee, which she took off to the side and guzzled. The rhythm of her morning bakery routine set in and provided some level of comfort.

"Music?" Andy asked.

"Yes! Let's hear some classic rock today."

He found a station on the satellite radio, and soon, Springsteen's "Thunder Road" was playing. The familiarity of the song helped Stella relax more.

Once they were set up for the day, Stella went to her office. She checked her email to see if Mary or one of the others wrote. There was only a quick email from Elly that read, "Everything will be okay, Stella."

As the morning progressed, Stella returned to questioning the decision to wait until tomorrow. Around noon, she returned to her office and decided to work on some book orders. It wasn't long before Andy yelled back down the hallway, "Stella! Get out here."

Stella came out and looked in the direction Andy was pointing to find Mary on the sidewalk in front of the bakery. She was slowly making her way to the door, wearing a bright fuchsia scarf with an orange stripe over a yellow dress. Her small frame wrapped in an unusual burst of color stepped inside. She walked up to Stella.

"Can we go talk in your office?" Mary asked her.

They got to Stella's office, where Stella closed the door and took off her apron, hanging it on a hook. She started to feel warm. Instead of sitting at her desk, she sat in one of the chairs for guests next to Mary and turned the chair to face her. She noticed Mary was wearing cherry red sandals and wondered what all the colors were about—fuchsia, orange, yellow, and red. It wasn't that Mary didn't wear colorful clothing, but this was extravagant.

Stella waited for Mary to speak, but when she didn't, she started. "We've all missed you, Mary. I didn't mean to intrude by going to your home. I'm sorry. I only—"

"Stop, Stella," Mary said.

Stella had the palms of her hands resting on her thighs. Mary reached over and placed one of her hands on top of Stella's. It made her remember the last time their hands touched as they stood next to Commander, the large white wolf at the sanctuary.

"I'm the one who owes you and everyone an apology," Mary continued. "As you know, I've led a solitary life in many ways since Don passed on. The friendships I now have with you and the others are gifts. You bring me joy. The bakery brings me joy. Joy and happiness and a sense of belonging I didn't realize was missing. I've been overwhelmed with something, and I have acted poorly."

Stella wondered what it could all mean. Where was she going with this? She waited, leaning slightly forward and looking intently at Mary. She could see Mary had applied thick foundation to try to hide the dark circles beneath her eyes.

"I'm sorry for the way I behaved when you came to my home. It won't happen again. You are always welcome." Mary gently squeezed Stella's hand and let go. She unwrapped the fuchsia scarf from around her neck. It fell into her lap and gathered there against her yellow dress like an art object. "I have a story to tell you," Mary said. "Do you have time?"

Mary and Stella stayed in the small office for over two hours. Mary talked, and Stella mostly listened. Mary told her about the breast cancer diagnosis she'd received after they returned from Montana. She had already started chemotherapy.

"It doesn't look good," she told Stella, "but I've made a decision to commit my all to the treatment."

She explained about the fear, anxiety, and loneliness she had experienced since their trip, yet she couldn't bring herself to ask for help. She didn't know what was holding her back. Seeing Stella at her home broke something free within Mary and allowed her to move forward. She had good energy the next morning, so she set out on an adventure before arriving at the bakery.

"Does your clothing have to do with your adventure?" Stella asked.

"It does," Mary said. "I went to see one of my husband's homes."

"What do you mean?" Stella asked.

"You may remember that he was just starting out as an architect when the accident happened," Mary explained. She took in a deep breath, and Stella watched her chest expand beneath the yellow fabric. "But he started with so much enthusiasm and potential. He left three completed homes when he died. Magical homes. Similar to Eichlers with the tall windows, but cozier inside. Wood over concrete. Alcoves for small gatherings. And his signature feature: treehouses."

"Treehouses?"

"Yes." Mary's cheeks started to glow as she talked. Even in her condition, this memory broke through to bring color to her face. "Each house had a magnificent treehouse in the back yard. Something for children, for sure, but large enough for a small family to gather in."

"That's really something," Stella said.

"So, today," Mary continued, fingering the soft fabric of her scarf, "I got dressed in the brightest outfit I could put together and drove to one of the houses. In La Habra Heights."

Mary went on to explain what happened when she arrived. A

woman was home. Mary explained who she was. It turned out the woman and her husband were the original owners. She let Mary in. Almost intuitively, she gave her space to walk about. Mary delighted in seeing the original wood floors. She ran her hands along the cabinetry in the kitchen, touching the original fixtures. She examined an alcove off the living room where numerous plants had been arranged on a built-in shelving unit near a window. Magazines in a wicker basket rested up against a reading chair. Then she stood with her small body within the frame of the expansive windows, looking out toward the back yard. It looked weathered, but the treehouse still stood.

"We've had to make repairs over the years," the woman told Mary, coming up behind her and gesturing toward the treehouse. "It has required a good amount of maintenance, but we love it."

"Do you use it?" Mary asked.

"Not much in recent years," the woman said. "Our children have left and started their own families, but when they were small and even throughout their teen years, they were always up there."

Hearing children had played in the treehouse made Mary's eyes water. She imagined how it would have sounded from the kitchen.

"Would you like to go out?" the woman asked.

Mary was alone in the back yard. A path led to the treehouse. She looked up at the structure. It was peaceful, resting within and below the tree's magnificent canopy. She tested the ladder. Gathering her balance and steadying her shaking knees, Mary made her way up.

Once she was inside the treehouse, she wept. She touched her left breast and placed the palm of her hand over her heart. She took off her red sandals to feel the floor of the treehouse on her soles. There were three windows and a skylight. Mary lay down beneath the skylight on her back and extended her arms, seeing the blue sky between leaves and branches.

Although Mary stayed there for a while, the woman never bothered her. It was there, within one of Don's beloved creations,

Mary felt herself opening up more. Something expanded in her chest, in her heart. She let herself fully feel the memories and emotions she rarely dipped her toes into. And her most private secret was on her mind.

There in the treehouse, she recalled what had happened over two decades before.

Mary's memory went back to a few years after Don died. She had been busy getting along building her professional life, throwing herself into her career to help wear off the shock of Don's passing and the abrupt end to their planned future. She started to find her life satisfying, except for the occasional hollow feeling that appeared from time to time. Regularly traveling to attend and present at conferences while starting her private practice, Mary devoured the literature of her field and believed she had found her calling. This belief provided her solace and helped to keep the hollowness at bay.

One spring, she attended a two-day symposium on the intersection of spirituality and psychology. It was held in a retreat-style setting at the Sisters of St. Joseph in the city of Orange, just a few miles from her home. Mary was greeted at the symposium by a woman named Anne. She checked Mary and the others in, providing them with programs and name badges. Mary sat through the early sessions enjoying the discussions and recognized a few acquaintances in the audience. She looked around from time to time to see if she could spot any nuns. If there were any there, they must be an order who didn't wear habits. Mary took to speculating on a few women during one session that dragged on a little too long. Then it was lunchtime.

A buffet was set up. Mary went down the line stacking her plate high with mashed potatoes and a goulash of some sort. "It's a Hungarian family recipe from Sister Agnes," she overheard a woman setting up trays and silverware tell another attendee. Mary placed water and a cookie on her tray and decided to head outside. She found a place off from the others. It was warm out, and the grounds were peaceful. She was scanning the program to read more about the afternoon sessions when a woman appeared. It was the woman named Anne who had checked everyone in.

"May I join you?" she asked Mary.

Although she was enjoying the quiet and solitude, Mary made a gesture toward her table and said, "Of course."

Anne sat down and started on her goulash. "Oh! So delicious," she said to Mary. "I've had it several times, and it's always good. You know, the spices."

"Yes, it is tasty," Mary replied. "So, you work here? With the nuns?"

"I do," Anne said. "I'm the activities manager. Going on five years. I love it."

They were silent for a while, eating their food.

"I'm interested in the talk later today on crone wisdom," Anne told Mary.

"Really? That's curious. You seem so young. Why does that interest you?" Mary asked.

The woman laughed. "How old do you take me for?"

Mary looked carefully at Anne's face. With her focus, she noticed small lines starting around her mouth and eyes she didn't notice before. She wasn't sure what to guess and didn't want to offend the woman.

Anne looked directly into Mary's eyes, making Mary put her focus back on her stew and potatoes. She could sense Mary growing uncomfortable, so she let her off the hook.

"I'm forty-five."

"I see," Mary replied. She wasn't sure what else to say, and she sensed Anne was looking at her and waiting. Then Mary started, "So, the crone?"

"Right," Anne said. "I've always found a wisdom in certain older women, but age is only one factor. It has to do with having a life well-lived. You can never be too young to get started with that."

This gave Mary pause. The phrase "a life well-lived" hung in the air. She wondered if she was on that path but quickly moved any question from her mind. "Well, that sounds right to me," was all she said to Anne.

"Yeah, so, the other thing is that I could use some wisdom now," Anne told her, resting her fork on her plate.

"Are you facing a big decision?" Mary asked.

"No," Anne said. "I guess you could say I'm at a crossroads. Mending a broken heart."

Mary felt something deep inside and knew it was the hollow feeling being stirred up. "I'm sorry to hear that," she told her. "Was it a long relationship?"

"Yes," Anne said. "Eight years. I guess like with a lot of people, I thought I was set for life. You know, companionship. The whole thing."

Mary felt the stirring again. She thought it would be best to move on to a new topic, but she couldn't help herself. "Where is he now?" she asked.

Anne turned toward Mary. Her eyes were watery. Mary knew the look well from her therapy practice and her own face she had seen often in the mirror.

"Her name was Janet," Anne said. "She moved to Texas. I hear outside of Austin."

Mary didn't offer any information about Don and her life. After lunch, she returned to her seat in the large room. When the talk on crone wisdom started, she looked around and located Anne sitting off on the side with her notebook in hand.

The next day at the symposium followed a similar pace. In the morning, it was Anne again at the table greeting the attendees and answering any questions. Mary politely said hello.

Anne smiled at Mary. She had one of those childlike smiles that made her whole mouth open and her eyes widen. It was hard to not return a smile to such an open face. *Maybe that is why I took her for younger*, Mary thought. Something about Anne's face, her mouth, her open smile and eyes, made Mary think she would not have a broken heart for long. Everything about her had resiliency and enthusiasm.

"Mary," Anne started, "would you like to have lunch together again? I would love to know your thoughts on the crone wisdom talk yesterday."

Mary wasn't sure. Not wanting to appear rude, she responded, "I'd love to."

The buffet offered another goulash, but this time with rice. It turned out to be just as delicious. One thing Mary was never ashamed of was how much she liked to eat. She piled her plate high again and made her way to the same table outside. Anne was already sitting there.

Mary joined Anne, and they started a conversation while eating. Somehow, it seemed familiar to Mary. While Anne talked, Mary watched, seeing more that she hadn't noticed the day before. Anne's hair was chestnut brown with some strands here and there of a warm honey color. These strands appeared like tiny lights under the sun and were complemented by Anne's linen blouse. The blouse was a shade of blue Mary had a hard time remembering the name of, and then it came to her: periwinkle. And she noticed Anne's hands. They were elegant with long fingers. Somehow, her hands seemed delicate yet strong. Then there was the smile she offered to Mary several times over lunch. Mary took it all in, surprised by how she felt, as if Anne's enthusiasm had easily transferred over to her.

Before the day concluded, Mary and Anne exchanged phone numbers. Within a few days, the calls started. They met several times for dinner over the next six months and quickly developed a deep connection. It was the first time since Don's passing that Mary had started to let someone in. Anne became a bright light in her life. She felt she had something to look forward to and someone to share stories with about her work.

Because of Mary's travel schedule, they also spent a good amount of time talking on the phone with a long stretch of miles between them. The women looked forward to their conversations, so much so that Mary even made a ridiculously expensive long-distance call once from a hotel room in Boston. It was during that call that Anne revealed, "I like you, Mary."

Mary was surprised. She responded, "I like you too. I'm so happy about our friendship."

There was silence on other end of the line, and then Anne said, "I'm not sure you understand, Mary. I like you not just as a friend. I like you more."

Mary's hold on the phone became shaky. She could feel her neckline getting sweaty. Don immediately came into her mind. She abruptly ended the call and lay back on her hotel bed.

That night, Mary couldn't sleep. She would need to kindly tell Anne such a relationship would never be. But that was not what happened. At least, not initially.

When Mary returned from Boston, she went over to Anne's. Anne was renting a small cottage on the property of a large house not too far from the Sisters of St. Joseph. Behind the cottage, she had a small garden of wildflowers and rosemary she tended to.

When Anne answered the door, she was wearing the periwinkle blouse, her hair pulled back to reveal small silver hoop earrings. They went to a bench near the garden. Mary was nervous and felt the sweaty feeling starting. She was about to start telling Anne how she felt and that a romance between them could never be when Anne kissed her. At first, Mary didn't resist. Her heart pounded and her stomach tossed around. She felt dizzy. Then she pulled away.

"This can't be," she told Anne.

"Why?" Anne asked her.

"Because . . ." Mary started slowly, trying to find the right thing to say. "Anne . . . I'm not a lesbian."

Anne's face opened into one of her smiles. "What does that have to do with it?" she asked Mary.

"Anne, I was married to my husband. My life partner," she said, feeling nervous. "I'm sorry if I somehow led you on."

"Led me on?" Anne laughed. "Who are you fooling, Mary? I know you feel it too."

Mary looked at Anne. Her heart was beating so loudly she was sure Anne could see it through her shirt. Then she looked away.

She did feel it, but she resisted. She got up and left.

Anne called out to her, "Mary, don't go! Please stay. Let's talk," but Mary walked to her car, got in, and drove home. She sat on her couch and cried, feeling confused and afraid. She kept recalling the kiss. Throughout the day, as she recalled it, she realized she was feeling more and more aroused. As she became more aroused, her fear heightened. She felt her life had been disrupted.

Anne didn't want to let Mary go. She was able to get Mary to meet with her on several more occasions, but Mary could not allow herself to love Anne as she wanted.

"What is it, Mary?" Anne asked, standing in Mary's kitchen. "Is it because of Don?"

"Partly," she told Anne, "but it is also me. I'm not ready for this."

"You're not ready for love?"

"It's not just love, Anne," Mary told her. "It's a whole thing. A whole thing I'm not ready for."

Anne waited and then decided to tell Mary what she believed. "You let something close when you lost Don. It doesn't need to stay this way, Mary."

"You don't understand," Mary told her. "You don't understand what it was like with Don."

"I want to understand," Anne said. "Let me understand." Anne came close to Mary and put her arms around her. "Mary, I love you."

The words opened up a longing within Mary, but she was not able to go there. She allowed herself to feel as much as she could until she closed part of herself off. She let Anne hold onto her for a few minutes, but then she moved her away and asked her to leave.

After Anne left, Mary cried on and off for a few weeks. She didn't return Anne's calls, and then they stopped. *This was only a few months of my life*, Mary finally told herself to minimize Anne and the experience in comparison to the years with her husband. *And a woman?* she would also think to make it seem like an impossibility. She went on with her life, as she did after Don passed, pouring herself into her work. Over the years, Anne was a memory that could be recalled, but Mary never allowed herself to spend much time there. She never spoke of her with anyone.

It wasn't until Mary received the cancer diagnosis that Anne returned with a force in her mind. She began to look for Anne online but found nothing. The search for her became a preoccupation, the only thing that could take her mind off the cancer and what felt like endless medical appointments during which her body was poked and turned into something inanimate. Mary remembered the longing she'd felt when Anne professed her love and put her arms around her. Anne represented something good and true she had turned away from. She believed that if she found out what became of Anne, she would achieve something like closure. Maybe peace. Mary began to feel guilt and remorse for how she had treated her. And then there was the terrible feeling of regret she was struggling with. *Where is Anne?* was the question that plagued Mary.

After not finding any leads online, Mary called the Sisters of St. Joseph. She explained she was looking for an employee from twenty years ago.

"What did you say her name was?" a young voice asked Mary.

"Anne Robertson," Mary said. Hearing the name spoken out loud in her own voice after so many years brought tears to her eyes. "Anne Robertson," she told the young voice again.

She explained to Mary that they would need to look into it more. "Perhaps one of the older sisters will know something."

And then, within a few days, Mary received a call. It was the same young voice on the line. She had a name and number for someone named Anne Thomas who lived in Denver, Colorado, and was willing to talk with Mary.

When Mary made the call, a woman who identified herself as

Susan answered. "Oh, yes, Mary," Susan said. "Anne has been waiting for your call."

And then Anne was there.

"Hi, Mary," she said.

Mary found it hard to compose herself. She was overcome with emotion. The medications and cancer treatments made her body old and tired, but in this moment, when she heard Anne's voice, she felt very alive and relieved. She had found her. Mary sobbed while Anne waited.

"Take your time, Mary," Anne said. "I was always hoping for this moment."

Mary discovered Anne left her job with the Sisters of St. Joseph after a few years and decided to go back to school. She moved to where her parents lived outside of Denver and started taking art classes. She was a potter and printmaker with substantial success. Anne had been married for twelve years to Susan Thomas, a restaurant owner.

"Guess what my studio is called?" she asked Mary.

"I have no idea," Mary said.

"Oh, it will ring a bell, I'm sure. It's called Crone Cottage."

Mary laughed the most she had since starting her treatments.

Once their conversation had taken on a rhythm and Mary felt safe, she let out something she only then realized she had a deep desire to say. "Anne, all those years ago, I want you to know . . . I loved you too."

"Oh, Mary," Anne said, "I knew that."

They talked for several hours. Mary told her about her life, which she realized must have sounded the same as it did twenty years ago. But then she told her about the Wild Librarian, the book club, the travels.

"What!" Anne yelled through the phone. "Now, this sounds great! Women Who Run With the Wolves Book Club. I love it!"

Near the end of the call, Anne waited for the right moment to say it. "Mary, this is your time."

"What do you mean?"

"This is your time for love. To allow yourself to feel love again. Do for yourself what I'm sure you would tell your clients," Anne told her.

Mary was silent on the other end of the line. She looked down at her feet. Even her feet had aged.

"The bakery. Those women in the book club. Your dear friends. You are not alone. Mary, your community is waiting."

In a few days, Mary received a package in the mail from Colorado. Inside was an older issue of *Studio Potter* magazine featuring Anne on the cover. Mary read the article on Anne, taking in the photos of her and her studio. In one photo, Anne stood holding a vase in her elegant hands. One of her vibrant prints was on the wall behind her. Her hair was short, in a pixie cut. Mixed in with her grays were some remaining hints of chestnut and honey. And there was the large smile Mary remembered. *What was it that she said?* Mary tried to recall, and then she did. *Ah, yes*, she told herself, *it is there in that face and that smile—what she aspired to all those years ago: a life well-lived.*

There was also a piece of paper inside the envelope. It was a photocopy of a page from a book of Walt Whitman's poetry. The lines read like a cataloging and celebration of the various parts of the human body, including the womb, hips, and—yes—breasts. Whitman even included the nipples! Mary read through, feeling a calm aliveness moving through her as she reached the final lines:

O I think these are not the parts and poems of

the body only, but of the soul,

O I think these are the soul!

If these are not the soul, what is the soul?

Mary was still on the floor of the treehouse as she recalled her experiences. She thought of Don and how he had lived life with such passion. She imagined Anne maybe working on something today inside Crone Cottage. And then she remembered Stella's face in her front window. First, her face had looked worried and perplexed, but then, when Mary opened the door briefly, Stella's face had changed. It made Mary hesitate, but now she knew that what came across Stella's face was love. It was love that had brought her to Mary's home. She heard Anne's voice: "Your community is waiting."

Mary got up from the floor of the treehouse. She made a decision. She was going to live for as long as she could. Joyously. And in community.

She climbed down from the treehouse and made her way along the path barefoot. The woman opened the door and offered her an arm while Mary put her sandals back on. Her next stop on the agenda was the Wild Librarian.

In Stella's office, after Mary shared her story, they hugged for a long time and cried. Mary believed her heart was fully open and healed.

The Women Who Run With the Wolves quickly moved into action. They created a calendar for Mary's care. Grace and the Two A's were also part of the rotation.

At first, Mary responded well to the chemotherapy. She experienced few side effects but grew tired and depressed as it went on. Then a heavy sickness came and lasted through the remaining treatments. Eating became a chore, and trying to find something that gave Mary any trace of an appetite required patience and creativity. Only one thing never failed: Taos Bread. Mary would call the Wild Librarian when she was running low.

"Mary's on the line again!" It was often Grace calling out.

"Mary," Stella told her over the phone, "don't you think you need to eat more than the Taos Bread?"

Mary was quiet on the other end.

"How about I bring you some soup in a bit?"

"Soup. Yuck. I can't even stomach the thought. Just bread, please."

Even people who had never tried Stella's Taos Bread heard of it: oncologists, medical assistants, bathing nurses, Mary's primary care doctor. She let everyone know of its healing powers. "Without it, I would be eighty pounds," she said more than once. "I would have disappeared by now."

When Mary completed chemotherapy, her spirit remained intact, but her body was tired. Everything felt like a strain. Then she got the good news: no trace of the cancer. This gave her enough energy to return to sitting beneath the avocado tree in the mornings and even for an hour or so at her writing desk, where she perused journals and made notes. They held a celebration at the bakery. Afterward, Stella drove Mary home and walked her to the front door.

"Sometimes during all this," Mary said, "I thought of Robert."

"Robert?" Stella asked.

"Robert Gonzales," Mary continued. "The man whose wife ran off and left him. What was his wife's name?"

"Maria," Stella said.

"Right." Mary started digging in her purse for her keys. She opened the front door and paused. "I went out with a group twice to canvas—place flyers around with her photo."

"I remember all that very well," Stella said.

"I thought of Robert once I got sick," Mary told her. "I thought of how he seemed to get stuck in time, unable to change. It is very sad, but I understand. That almost happened to me."

Mary stepped inside, and Stella followed her. They sat on the couch in the front room. Dr. Freud came in and jumped on Mary's lap, arching his back when he felt the touch of her hand.

"I can understand why you thought of Robert," Stella said. "For different reasons, your lives changed overnight."

"Yes." Mary touched the tip of Dr. Freud's tail. "They certainly did."

"We are all so different though," Stella said, sad as she thought of Robert. "We never know how we will really act until something is upon us.'

"There's a saying I use with some of my clients," Mary said. "How funny I forgot about it until this moment."

"What is it?"

"Give me a second." Mary looked off into a corner of the room. "Yes, that's it!" She raised her finger up as if she were touching something in the air. Stella waited. Mary turned her focus back to her and spoke the words slowly. "We must be willing to give up the life we've planned so we can have the life that's waiting for us."

"Wow." Stella took a deep breath. "That's beautiful, Mary."

"I th nk I got it right! Well, close enough." She laughed. "I believe it's a Joseph Campbell quote."

They sat together without speaking for a moment. The house was quiet except for Dr. Freud's soft purr.

"Do you ever talk to Robert still?" Mary asked Stella.

"Oh. yes," Stella told her. "Not long conversations like in the past, but he comes in often. Mostly in the mornings."

"My parents have been gone for many years," Mary said, jumping to another topic. It was something she frequently did during and after the chemotherapy. Stella thought of Mary's new way of conversing as a collage, as if she were piecing unrelated things together yet they were part of a whole. "My parents had cancer," she said, "just like me."

"I remember you sharing that with us," Stella said. "And that is how I also lost my parents."

"Yes," Mary continued while looking down at Dr. Freud. "My parents remained in mainland China. I was only to come to the U.S. for college, but then I met Don and we made our home here."

"Did you get a chance to visit your parents?" Stella asked.

"Yes, many times, actually. I miss them. It was just the three of us, and we were close. Even from a distance I felt close to them." Mary moved her legs, and Dr. Freud stood and stretched his paws in front of him before returning to a ball shape on Mary's lap. "I considered moving back after Don died," she told Stella. "You know, back to

China. But my work and wanting to stay where Don and I lived kept me here." She started tracing circles with her fingers on Dr. Freud's head. He purred in response.

Mary's eyes grew heavy as if she were falling asleep from her own storytelling. Stella waited and then spoke softly.

"Mary, would you like me to help you get ready for bed?"

She moved in her seat. "Oh, no, I'll be okay. You should get going," she told Stella.

Mary walked Stella to the front door.

"Stella, when I was telling you all that, I didn't mean to ramble." She gave a warm smile.

"Not at all," Stella said.

"What I was getting at is that I'm so thankful I was able to change. Having all of you at this time—what a blessing." She lingered at the door with Stella. "It's because I opened up. I opened up and moved forward with life. I wish the same for Robert."

Mary stood at the door with her hand on the doorknob. She looked at Stella and then toward the tree in her front lawn until her gaze landed on the moon.

"You did," Stella told her. "You really did. Mary, we're all so proud of you."

Mary decided to terminate the lease on her office that she had retained throughout her treatment. It kept hope and possibility open, but then practical matters, especially finances, took over.

"If I get my strength back," she told the others, "I could use my front room in the house as an office." But it would never come to be, and Mary's practice folded. "And so it is," she said to Dr. Freud. "We are moving into retirement earlier than planned."

Several of her clients came to see her, made phone calls, or wrote emails, including clients from many years ago who heard of Mary's retirement. She considered the visits, calls, and messages blessings. She knew she had impacted others, but these affirmations felt like a beautiful and sturdy net she could now rest her tired body on.

Within a few months, the cancer reappeared, but in her other breast. It started all over again—the chemotherapy, the rotating help from the book club and Wild Librarian staff, the depression, and the sickness. Mary embarked upon her journey weaker this time though, and one afternoon in between treatments, she suffered a mild stroke while in her bed with only Dr. Freud as a witness. Sheila and Barbara found her later in the evening. After several days in the ICU and a few more in the hospital while she stabilized, Mary returned home.

"Ladies," Mary told the book club as she sat in her bed, propped up by several pillows, "some tough things in life we can't overcome, and others we can. I've accepted that."

No one said anything. Stella nodded. Elly sighed. Barbara and Sheila were sitting on opposite sides of Mary's bed, each of them holding one of her hands.

"I have an important question for you all to consider. Who will take care of Dr. Freud? Knowing his future whereabouts will bring me peace."

The discussion of Mary's cat was an important and anxious one over the next few days. None of the women could take him for different reasons. They needed to find a resolution and report back to Mary to bring her comfort, so they were thankful when the Two A's stepped up. Mary was pleased with the resolution. From that moment, she declined rapidly over the next week. Arrangements were made for home hospice care.

It was quiet in Mary's room. Dr. Freud was curled in a ball at her feet when Stella arrived. A nurse was wiping Mary's forehead with a cloth. She left the room, saying she would be in the living room if anything was needed.

Mary looked tiny on the bed, except for her belly. Stella could see how it was horribly distended beneath the covers like a large lump. She remembered how her mom's stomach had taken on this shape at the end of her struggle with cancer too, as if fluids were held up there and no longer moving smoothly through the body. Mary was resting on a blue pillow, her hair a gray halo framing her small face. In the window across from her bed, directly in Mary's line of vision, the old avocado tree stood in the sun. She'd had the Two A's move her bed and furniture around several weeks ago so she could see the tree whenever she wanted. They'd even surprised her by hanging a string of cafe lights within its branches, allowing the tree to comfort Mary throughout the night.

When Mary started to speak, Dr. Freud yawned and stretched his front paws. "I imagine something," she said with her eyes half-closed and looking toward the ceiling.

"What is it?" Stella asked.

Mary closed her eyes for several seconds and opened them, now looking sleepily at Stella. Then she looked again at the ceiling.

"Mary, do you see something up there?"

"Yes, a goddess spaceship."

Stella was not expecting this.

"It's white. Glowing. Hovering far up in the sky above the house," Mary explained. She seemed to fall asleep, but then her eyes opened again.

"They are going to send down a thread. A golden thread to pick me up," she told Stella.

"That sounds beautiful, Mary. Are you afraid at all?" Stella asked.

"I'm not," she said. "There are people waiting for me."

"People you know?"

"Some of them." She was quiet again, and then her eyes opened wider. "My parents," she said, smiling.

Stella took a seat next to Mary's bed. Several things were gathered on a small table near her. Stella looked at what was there: Mary's watch, her cell phone, a glass of water, the nurse's cloth, an old photograph of Mary with her husband, another of Dr. Freud as a kitten in a younger and more vibrant Mary's arms, and a small ceramic bowl containing Commander's white fur. Stella remembered how the fur had looked when she first saw it grouped in Mary's hands. She imagined Commander at this moment in Montana, walking deliberately over the tall, thick grass in full possession of his majestic body. She could recall his howl in her memory as if she just heard it yesterday.

"Don is there," Mary said.

"Don is in the goddess spaceship?" Stella asked.

"He is."

Dr. Freud walked a few steps up on the bed and put his head under Mary's hand. Stella saw her fingers move slightly to pet him, and even this light movement made him loudly purr.

Stella closed the bakery the morning of Mary's funeral service. All the staff wanted to attend. Several people still met there first in the morning, including Barbara, Sheila, Elly, Grace, and Andy. Anne and Susan flew in from Colorado. Per Mary's request, Stella had called Anne to let her know of Mary's passing.

Holy Family Cathedral was a long walk from the Wild Librarian, but everyone felt inspired to do it. In the spirit of Mary's clothing the day she came to the bakery to tell Stella of her diagnosis, Stella had asked everyone to wear bright colors. They walked as a rainbow down the old Santa Ana sidewalks into the city of Orange.

It was a warm morning and the time of year when jacaranda trees bloomed with their striking flowers. As they made their procession, the sidewalks were covered in fallen blossoms, making a purple, sticky carpet. By the time they arrived at the steps of the cathedral, the soles of their shoes had a layer of the flowers attached, and purple blossoms here and there peppered their hair.

The book club returned to their regular schedule in two months. Stella made a large loaf of Taos Bread. Sheila, Elly, Barbara, and Stella met thirty minutes before the advertised time in Stella's office to have a moment of silence for Mary, but nothing about the evening turned out to be somber. In fact, it took on more of a party feel. They all agreed they could feel Mary's presence.

As they made their way back to the main bakery floor, they found three young women at a table. "Are you the Women Who Run With the Wolves?" one of them asked. They laughed, and Barbara let out a howl.

"We are the group!" Elly said.

"How wonderful to have new members," Barbara told them.

They discussed Estés' work in *The Joyous Body* and got to the part where the bodies of women are understood as trees. They talked about the wisdom of an old tree with its scars and brokenness, yet its strong and unwavering trunk could withstand many storms.

"I just thought of Mary and her avocado tree," Elly said. "Remember how important it was for her at the end—that she could see it whenever she wanted?"

"Yes," Sheila said. "She would really love what we are discussing."

"Who's Mary?" one of the young women asked.

Elly, Barbara, Sheila, and Stella looked at each other. It was silent. Then Grace's voice could be heard several feet away talking to a customer. They heard the metal clang of the cash register drawer. Stella cleared her throat, indicating she was going to speak. They all waited to see what she would say.

"Mary Chin was a shining star," she said. "A miracle who lived right here in Santa Ana. She was one hell of a woman."

Taos Bread
Recipe for 12 muffins

2 cups unbleached organic flour

1 can (15 ounces) pumpkin puree

3/4 cup organic raw sugar

1/3 cup unsweetened applesauce

2–3 teaspoons cinnamon

1/3 cup almond milk

1 teaspoon ginger

1 1/2 teaspoons organic vanilla extract

1 teaspoon baking soda

1/4 cup diced or chopped organic walnuts

1 teaspoon baking powder

1/4 cup diced or chopped organic pecans

1/2 teaspoon salt

a little extra raw sugar and pecans to sprinkle on top

Preheat oven to 350 degrees. Mix together the flour, sugar, cinnamon, ginger, baking soda, baking powder, and salt. Once combined well, mix in all the wet ingredients: pumpkin puree, unsweetened applesauce, almond milk, and vanilla. After mixing your batter (make sure not to overmix), stir in the walnuts and pecans. Scoop the batter into your baking cups. Before putting the muffins in the oven, sprinkle a little sugar and pecan pieces on top. Bake for 20–25 minutes. To make sure the muffins are ready, insert a toothpick near the center of one. If the toothpick comes out clean, you know they are done! If any batter sticks to the toothpick, they need to bake for longer.

PERFECT PAIRING: For writers looking for inspiration, Stella recommends Natalie Goldberg's *Writing Down the Bones* as you enjoy your Taos Bread. For everyone, Goldberg's memoir *Long Quiet Highway* is a delight. You may also consider looking through a book of Georgia O'Keeffe's paintings to experience her New Mexico influence while you devour your bread. If you're feeling a bit decadent, eat your Taos Bread warmed with a scoop of coconut or vanilla ice cream on top. Yes!

Judy's Bread
Recipe for 1 regular-size loaf

1 3/4 cup unbleached organic flour
1/4 teaspoon baking soda
1/2 cup organic raw sugar
1/2 teaspoon salt
1 teaspoon cinnamon
3 tablespoons coconut oil
1/4 teaspoon clove
3/4 cup sweet potato puree
1/4 teaspoon nutmeg
3/4 cup almond milk
2 teaspoons baking powder
1 teaspoon apple cider vinegar

Preheat oven to 365 degrees. Get your loaf pan ready by lining it with parchment paper or spraying the interior with a nonstick cooking spray, such as olive oil spray. In a small bowl, mix the almond milk together with the apple cider vinegar. Set the small bowl aside. In a large bowl, mix together all the dry ingredients. Once the dry ingredients are mixed well, add the milk mixture, sweet potato puree, and coconut oil. Make sure the coconut oil is melted like a liquid before adding. The batter can be a little stiff, which is fine for a bread. If it is thin like a cake batter that you can easily pour, add a little bit of flour to stiffen it up. Put all the batter into your loaf pan. You are ready to place it in the oven. Wasn't that so easy? Bake for about 55 minutes. To make sure the bread is ready, insert a toothpick near the center of the loaf. If the toothpick comes out clean, the bread is done! If any batter sticks to the toothpick, place it back in the oven and check again every few minutes. This bread will be crumbly and difficult to evenly slice when it is still warm, so you may want to wait for it to fully cool. If you can't wait though, since it sure is delicious warm and fresh out the oven, cut yourself a crumbly slice to devour.

PERFECT PAIRING: See if you can find Judy Grahn's *Common Women Poems* through your library or a local used bookstore. Reading these lovely and sometimes gritty poems along with this hearty bread will make your heart soar as you realize what is "common" is actually magnificent. If you can't find these poems, check out one of Judy's more recent collections, such as *Love Belongs to Those Who Do the Feeling* (such a great title!).

The Pilgrim

Awoman wearing a hot pink dress wrapped in a bright red scarf with various baubles that sounded like wind chimes when she moved came into the Wild Librarian one morning while Stella was arranging freshly baked Taos Bread in the bakery case. The woman's hair, long and thick, was black like a raven and tousled. It was a few days shy of the one-year anniversary of Mary's passing, so Stella was heavily stocking Taos Bread throughout the week in her honor.

"Heeeellllllloooo," the woman called out to Stella in a sing-song voice. "Might you be the wild librarian?"

"I am," Stella responded.

The woman hummed and let out a sigh after taking in a deep breath full of the spices from the Taos Bread. She scanned Stella up and down, examining her oversize work shirt and old construction boots. Stella couldn't get a good read on the woman, but she didn't feel up to clever talk or a challenge without a second cup of coffee. She had been up too late talking on the phone, getting caught up on life with her brother, Ben, in Seattle. No challenge came from the woman though. Instead, she winked and stretched out her hand, causing several baubles to set off chimes.

"I'm Rita Johansen, another wild librarian."

Rita arranged her scarf back around her. Stella noticed there was a light thread of something that resembled tinsel woven here and there. It was quite beautiful. Then, as she looked down, she noticed the woman was barefoot. She would need to say something about this.

"What do you recommend for my first visit?" Rita asked while looking at the baked goods.

"For you," Stella said, "I'm thinking of a sampler plate. Go take a seat and I'll bring something over." She looked at Rita's feet and was about to comment when Rita stopped her.

"My apologies! I can sometimes get carried away and forgetful." She pulled sandals from a large book bag, slipped them on, and made her way to an open seat at the community table.

"My God," Rita said, digging her fork into the assortment Stella brought her. She pointed. "This! This! What is this divine thing?"

Stella laughed. It was her latest creation, made in honor of June Jordan's poetry collection *Directed by Desire*.

"That is the Rose Pistachio Desire Cupcake inspired by the phenomenal poet and activist June Jordan."

"I'm not familiar with her," Rita said, "but I've never tasted something this good."

"More?" Stella asked.

"Hell yes. Six in a to-go box. My colleagues are going to flip."

Stella discovered Rita was an archivist and rare book cataloger at a university in Los Angeles, but she had recently moved only a few miles from the Wild Librarian. After her first visit, Rita was so pleased with Stella's place that she started dropping in a few times each month, sometimes purchasing a dozen muffins or cupcakes to take to her librarian colleagues. She became an infrequent member of the Women Who Run With the Wolves Book Club, telling them, "Don't count on me as a regular. I like to dip in and out of things." During some visits, she would sit with Stella and talk about the world of libraries or a good book one of them was reading, but Rita's favorite topic was always men.

If Rita wasn't talking about a specific man, she was usually still talking about men in general, sex with men, or what she called her "erotic life." She had a curious fascination with the writer Henry Miller and could recite long passages from his works, especially *Crazy Cock* and *Tropic of Cancer*. Stella surrendered to Rita's demands one day and purchased several of Miller's titles, excluding *Crazy Cock*, which she put for sale in the Anais Nin section. "Only as an experiment," she told Rita. 'We'll see how he does here." When Rita suggested a new book-themed treat, Stella laughed but outright refused to make a *Crazy Cock* cupcake. "Children come in here!" she told her.

During one stop on her way to work at the university, Rita stood with her morning coffee while watching Stella make some repairs to a moon garland she had recently hung from the Wild Librarian's rafters. She took it down to spread it out on a table and add some jute thread to make the string stronger. Stella didn't notice until that moment how the garland bore some resemblance to Rita's scarves with the metallic threads and jangling objects.

"Did that thing come with all that glitter on it?" Rita asked, pointing to some of the crescent moon shapes that were covered in silver sparkles.

"No," Stella said. "I added it."

"Huh." Rita shook her head. "Stella Peabody. I think you're an odd bird like me."

"I was just thinking the same thing."

As the brief conversations between them added up and the women started to look forward to their encounters, some striking differences were also revealed. Stella had been in several long relationships, mostly earlier in life, but the closest she had come to marriage was living with a boyfriend for a few years in her thirties. She had been what she called "blissfully single" for well over a decade. In contrast, Rita had cruised through countless men and four husbands.

It made sense to Stella that Rita had been married four times and that each marriage had lasted less than three years. She was impulsive with men, got bored easily, and was difficult to hold onto.

Still, Rita swore to Stella that her last marriage to an English professor named Carl was different. Unlike the others, her fourth had ended when her husband fell severely ill one day and died two months later from an infection.

"It really knocked the sun out of me for a while," Rita told Stella one morning while eating a rose pistachio cupcake. There was a lull in the morning busyness, so they were sitting together by the window at a table Robert Gonzales had just left.

"That's a man of few words," Rita said, pointing to Robert as he made his way down the sidewalk. There was a slight drizzle. Stella looked out the window and saw Robert pick up his pace and put his newspaper over his head.

"Yes, he wasn't always like that," Stella said. "It's a tragic story I'll share sometime. Tell me about Carl."

"So, Carl was different from the others. He taught American literature where I work. Incredibly passionate about books and teaching, I must say—a lovely and sensual man." She rubbed her hands together on her thighs and bent forward. "All my adventures now are fun at the moment, they give me some sparks, but they never come close to what we had."

"How long were you married?" Stella asked.

"Two years. Two blissful years. He satisfied me more than the other husbands combined. Shit, those jokers were forgettable before I even received the divorce papers back from the state."

Stella couldn't help but feel skeptical that Rita's marriage to Carl would have outlasted her roving eye, but Rita did seem sincere when professing her love.

"I was just a few weeks away from turning fifty when he died," Rita explained. "I went into a despair I had never experienced before. I felt ungrounded, like something was ready to shift beneath me and swallow me up. I once heard someone describe anxiety as being depression's best friend, but I never felt it until those days. I was so blue but had a hard time sitting still. Then I thought a short trip might help."

"Did you go somewhere?"

"I took medical leave from the university. I can't recall how it even got approved I was so spaced out at the time. I rented a van. It was a hideous green minivan. Dear God! You should have seen the heap of a thing!" Rita laughed, bringing her jeweled fingers together. "In the back, I had all kinds of food, drinks, clothes, and blankets. A carton of Marlboros. It was kind of my moving house for a week. I drove it up the coast to Big Sur. To visit the Henry Miller Library."

Rita went on to share that the drive on Highway 1 was something she had never attempted as an adult. Once on a trip with her mom at the wheel, when Rita was sixteen, they were in a crash on the dangerous, cliff-hugging road. She remembered being in a state of shock, her body quivering, while they waited for a tow truck to bring them back to where they lived outside Santa Barbara.

"I wanted to get up to the library so much over the years, but for all my wild ways and confidence I just didn't have it in me to do that winding road. Finally, I decided the time had come. Boy, was my stomach twisting and turning at first as I headed up in that old green jalopy." Rita took a sip of her coffee and then leaned far back in her chair with her arms extended out by her sides.

Stella couldn't help but notice the usual bob and flop of Rita's heavy breasts as she moved, and the curve of her round belly.

"It turned out not to be a big deal after all," Rita continued. "I think I was still too heartbroken to care. Maybe I thought the van would plunge off the side of one of those cliffs. The way I was feeling, I wouldn't have minded. As I said, I was ungrounded. Jesus. I can't say. All I knew was I thought the adventure would save me. That's not the right word though. I mean, it was an adventure, but it was deeper than that. More like a pilgrimage."

"Pilgrimage." Stella repeated the word out loud, feeling each letter.

"Yeah, 'Pilgrimage at Fifty' could be the title of it." She laughed a bit and looked out the window. The drizzle had become a light sun-shower. "So, my pilgrimage to Henry's library began on my fiftieth birthday. I wore my favorite blue dress with yellow flowers." She leaned in and whispered to Stella, "Not that this is a necessary part of the story, but I didn't wear panties the whole time. Shit!" She backed up in her chair and let out a wild cackle as her dark hair shook. "I was loose and ready for anything. My oblivion. I planned to sleep in the van near the library at one of the campgrounds."

"Hold on, Rita," Stella said. "I can tell this is going to be a good and long one. Let me grab some more coffee."

Stella came back with her work shirt tied around her waist, wearing a Wild Librarian T-shirt and holding a large cup. She sat at the table, leaning forward on her elbows. "Okay, let's go," she said.

"I took my time getting there. Up to Big Sur, that is. Four days. I would drive and then get out and walk around a bit. One day, I did some wine tasting at a classy vineyard and crashed out for several hours in their nicely manicured parking lot. Damn, what a mess I was! I must have looked like something from outer space pulling up in my green machine." Rita toyed with a decorative gold string that grouped below the "V" of the generous neckline of her dress.

"I didn't shower or even comb my hair those first four days. I mostly ate peanut butter sandwiches using a loaf of this amazing thick bread and a large jar of peanut butter from Bristol Farms. I was also into eating those chocolate donuts you can buy in a sleeve at a convenience store. Boy, those go great with black coffee in the morning. Maybe it's all the chemicals they use to make them that tricks your brain into thinking you're in paradise. I'd even dunk them while sitting in the van with the radio on."

"That actually sounds nice," Stella said, "like a complete escape from everything."

"It was definitely that. Sometimes, I parked in an ocean lot. I'd roll all the windows down and get in the back of the green machine, stretching out and listening to the waves, popping those small donuts one at a time into my mouth. Near Ragged Point, I slept most of the whole day away. Thinking back, I'm lucky nothing happened to me.

"I only had one book with me in the van. You know how unusual that is for me—I'm always carrying at least two in my tote bag everywhere I go. The weeks when Carl was sick and then after his death, I couldn't read, so I had this unusual book with me. It was *The Language of the Goddess*. Marija Gimbutas. I grabbed it from the bookshelf before I left home. I can't say why, but there is a magic with books. We both know that very well."

"Oh, yes. And I'm familiar with the book," Stella said. "I often have it in stock here."

"You know it's full of images then. Sometimes, I would leaf through it while in the van, scanning the images. There was one I kept returning to. It's odd what the brain goes to at times. It was a figure Gimbutas thought may represent a double goddess. It's symmetrical, showing two figures together. One has large breasts that hang like mine. I don't know, I just kept looking at it. It was somehow soothing."

Rita explained it was a warm day when she reached Big Sur. She stopped at a campground beforehand to comb the knots out of her hair and get cleaned up. "To make myself presentable for the moment," she said. She parked the green van along the side of the road by the Henry Miller Library. Everywhere she looked were redwoods.

"It was wondrous being there. You know what I mean. All the beauty of that place."

"Oh, yes," Stella said. She had been to Big Sur a few times over the years. Listening to Rita's story made her recall the scent of the redwoods and the magical, fairy-tale nature of the surroundings.

"So, I parked and walked up to the entrance. First, there was this outdoor art gallery of some type. Really crazy stuff on display. And then the house, which is really the library. It was just as I thought. Not pretentious. A tad messy here and there. But sensual. Welcoming. What I mean is . . . *relaxed*. Really divine." Rita stopped playing with the string on her dress and placed her hands on her thighs.

She told Stella she reached the deck in front of the library and found some other travelers. An old gray hippie couple from Colorado were enjoying a smoke, so Rita joined them. There was a young woman in a flowery dress like Rita, along with a few others. Everything glistened. It was a bit humid. Rita took her jacket off and used it to wipe away some water that had gathered on the seat of a white plastic chair. She sat in the chair and finished her cigarette. She had a cloth bag with her that included some supplies from the van. She ate a few spoonfuls of peanut butter straight from a jar and then sat back to gaze at the redwoods, the blue sky, and then the dirty soles of her feet. "Pilgrim's feet," she told Stella.

There were a few rows of chairs stretched across the lawn in front of the library beneath several strings of lights. She heard a man's voice say, "There was a wedding last night." Rita felt the scoop of peanut butter gather for a moment, but then it softened and filled her mouth in a satisfying way. She closed her eyes and felt sleepy. She let it all sink in, and when she was ready, she ventured into the library

It turned out the director of the library was inside. Rita described him as "good natured, a fine soul" to Stella. He was delighted to meet a librarian-loving Miller fan. She dramatically recited a few lines from *Crazy Cock* while acting out the words with her body, making the director and a few others inside the library laugh. Stella laughed as Rita stood in the Wild Librarian and performed a rendition.

"Now, get this," Rita began again. "After my little performance, I walked around. It's a small place inside, but there is stuff to look at everywhere. Postcards, photographs, and art hanging on the walls. I was looking through some books when I glanced up and saw a postcard stapled to a wood beam. It had an illustration of a simple pen drawing. I was stunned. The drawing mirrored the image, almost identically, of the double goddess from the Gimbutas book. I've always believed in synchronicity, but this was almost too much. Unfortunately, it wasn't for sale, but I spent several minutes just staring and tracing the image, first with my eyes and then with my finger." Rita put both her hands in the air, up high above her head, and made the image in the air for Stella, ending with her hands in her lap.

"I became aware of something at that moment," she told Stella. "First, I was so present in my body." She crossed her arms and ran her hands down her upper arms as if to illustrate something. "It was a strong awareness, mostly of my heart. It had an even beat. I was fifty years old, and even with all my bodily shenanigans, I can't recall ever being aware of this beating inside me. While in the library, I could hear it, and my movements were keeping time with the tempo."

A small group came into the bakery. Stella heard Andy greet them.

Rita paused and took an audible breath. "It wasn't just my heart," she told Stella. "It was my entire soul. Everything had an even beat."

"Hmm," Stella said. "So, what do you gather from it all? What did it mean?"

"Let me tell you—but first, some other things. Hold on, woman! Some stories take time."

Rita said the director had taken such a liking to her that he welcomed her to camp on-site, off to the side of the library. There, in the lush grass beneath the giant redwoods, Rita set up her tent. She stayed two nights. On the first night, she dreamed of the chairs on the lawn, the coastline, and the faces of the other travelers from the deck. When she awoke, she moved her feet against the soft interior of her sleeping bag and paused for a moment to see if she still felt the even beat. She did. Her whole body, she told Stella, had a smooth vibration. She could hear her heart. "Like a soft drum," she said. She walked around the library that day and into the small town, feeling her heart beating as she went. "I felt safe," she told Stella. "It was like I was moving toward something."

Rita went to a campsite and took a shower. She washed her hair using a bar of soap from her cosmetic bag. After drying off, she pulled her dress back on over her naked body. With her wet hair tied back with a rubber band, she made her way back to the library in motion with the beat. "Even my boobs danced along to this rhythm." She laughed.

As she walked, she picked up twigs, a few with leaves still attached, and constructed a wreath for her head. Then she was back at the library for the evening. She perused the books on sale again and bought a copy of Miller's *The Books in My Life*. The director was not there, but she had a long conversation with a cashier named Bob about Miller and her "pilgrimage." Bob was young, possibly still in his twenties.

"What started it? Your pilgrimage. Was there an event?" Bob asked.

"Yes," Rita said, touching the wreath around her head. "I lost someone important."

She slept soundly again that night. The next morning, she felt a rustling outside her tent and opened it to find several wild turkeys walking around the library. One, whom Rita took for an old, wise soul, looked at her in the tent. This was not her first time seeing a turkey up close. She always thought their eyes were beady, but this one had wonderful soft, peaceful eyes.

"Hello there," Rita said, and the turkey bent down to investigate something in the grass. Then he looked back at Rita before moving along with the others.

She made her way to the deck of the library and ate chocolate donuts she'd pulled from her van. The chairs that had been left for the wedding were now stacked off to the side. She gathered her dress in her lap and heard someone near her speaking: "Film festival?" Then, "Did you hear?" She looked over and saw it was Bob, the cashier from the day before, pouring a cup of coffee and talking to her. He had a cigarette dangling from his lips.

"I'm sorry?" Rita asked.

"We're going to have a film festival in two days. Will you be around still?"

"Oh, no," Rita told him, "I'm going to be heading out soon. Time to make my way home." She got up and walked over to pour herself a cup.

Rita studied the steam from her coffee in the cool morning air. It tasted delicious with her donuts. The turkeys from earlier appeared on the lawn.

"Well, look at that," Bob said. "I haven't seen them for a while."

Rita found the one with the peaceful eyes. He was slower than the others, or at least he enjoyed taking his time. She smiled and took a seat on the steps in front of the deck.

The turkeys walked around the lawn for several minutes until they disappeared into the redwoods. Bob came near Rita and leaned against a railing. He was holding a small plastic ashtray in the palm of his left hand.

"Opening soon?" Rita asked.

"Yep," Bob told her. He was curious. He looked young but talked and held his body like an older person. He put the ashtray down and used both of his hands to put his hair behind his ears. A few seconds passed. No one was around yet, and except for the occasional car it was silent. Rita took a few sips from her coffee.

"So, tell me something," Bob said. "Did you find what you were looking for?"

Rita loved the question. She closed her eyes and tilted her head back. She listened within herself and heard the soft drum. She knew it was her song. It sounded resilient, strong. She knew her story did not end with Carl and that she would be okay.

"I did," she told him. She put her coffee down and placed her right hand over her heart. "I'm going to take it all back home with me."

Stella delighted in Rita's pilgrimage story. It stayed on her mind for days. The next time Rita came in, Stella asked her to share the story with the Women Who Run With the Wolves Book Club at their next meeting.

Stella, along with the core members of the book club—Elly, Sheila, and Barbara—were joined by several others on the evening of Rita's storytelling. They made "pilgrimage" the overall theme for the night. Once Rita had finished her story, which engrossed and thoroughly entertained everyone, a young woman who identified herself as Victoria spoke. She told them she had gone on something she thought of as a feminist pilgrimage last summer. The women were quickly engrossed in another tale.

Unlike Rita's journey, Victoria had flown to New York to see a famous art installation at the Brooklyn Art Museum: Judy Chicago's *The Dinner Party*. She traveled solo and rented a tiny studio apartment for a week in the Greenpoint neighborhood. In between bites of a blueberry muffin, she shared about her time at the art museum and her various walks around Greenwich Village and to numerous bookstores.

"I had to ship several heavy boxes back to California," Victoria said. "They almost cost as much as my airfare."

"I think we have a lot in common, Victoria." Stella laughed.

Victoria's friend Manuela, who had accompanied her to the book club that night, then shared about a long journey she took to visit the town where most of her ancestors lived in Guatemala. She spoke about how it felt to reach the home where her great-grandparents once lived and sit inside the tiny church where they worshipped. "The lushness of the land," Manuela said, closing her eyes, "has always remained with me. I can still dream up the smells of the forest after a heavy rain."

"Will you return again?" Elly asked her.

"Oh, definitely." Manuela smiled. "I'm even considering moving there."

When Manuela finished, Barbara said, "Now that I've heard these stories, I realize we all went on pilgrimages." She pointed to Stella, Sheila, and Elly. "We just didn't call it that."

"You all went somewhere together?" Victoria asked.

"We certainly did. And Mary Chin was there too—our beloved friend who has since passed away."

"Where did you go?"

"Taos, New Mexico, to a wondrous lodge, and Bozeman, Montana, to stay at a wolf sanctuary."

"A wolf sanctuary!" Manuela laughed. "I've never heard of being able to vacation somewhere like that."

"I love New Mexico," Victoria said. "Let's hear your stories."

"Yes, I want to hear about all of this." Rita winked at Stella and the others.

Barbara looked around, receiving approval to share. "Well," she began, "we don't have time for both stories."

"Oh, sure we do!" a woman named Donna who had become an occasional member said. "We just need to get some more muffins first."

Everyone laughed, and the pilgrimage stories of New Mexico and Montana were shared after a second round of baked goods arrived.

When the evening ended, Rita came over to Stella. "Well, that was wonderful!" she told her.

"Just exceptional. And thank you for sharing your beautiful story, Rita."

"On another topic," Rita said, starting to gather her things, "do you accept book donations? I mean"—she pointed to the bookshelves—"to include here for sale along with the new books."

"Very rarely," Stella said. "You know how that is. It's just like at the library. People show up with musty old boxes from their garage of moldy things they should have tossed long ago."

Rita laughed. "So true!" She continued. "What I have though, of course, is a librarian's book collection. And an archivist at that." Rita could sense Stella was still hesitant. "Why don't you come over and see?" she offered. "It certainly won't hurt my feelings if you don't want anything. And bring Jane so I can meet her."

Rita's home was in the coveted Floral Park neighborhood of Santa Ana on Heliotrope Drive. It resembled one of several grand old Los Angeles neighborhoods. Coming across it often surprised people who were not expecting such vintage splendor in the heart of Orange County.

Stella pulled in front of Rita's 1920s storybook-style cottage. She parked and opened the back door for Jane to jump out. Jane walked over and began to sniff the lush grass.

"That's not a dog!" Rita called out to Stella, closing her front door behind her. "That's more of a wolf!"

Stella laughed while Jane trotted along investigating. "My, my," she said, gesturing toward the house and street as Rita walked toward them in one of her flashy scarves full of baubles. "It looks like librarian jobs pay pretty well at the university these days."

"It's a dream, isn't it?" Rita said. "I was looking for a new place after losing Carl. I certainly wasn't planning to move from Los Angeles and deal with a long commute, but coming home to this is worth it."

Hearing Rita mention Carl reminded Stella of an earlier conversation they'd had about money from an insurance policy that had helped Rita considerably following his passing. She realized this may have been how she bought the home. Stella felt foolish to have made such a careless comment, but Rita didn't seem upset as her breasts swayed back and forth while she happily moved toward Stella and embraced her.

They walked up the pathway to a rustic front door. Rita had a large crystal ball hanging from a braided rope outside near the entrance. It spun slightly in the wind, reflecting the sunlight. Stella was enchanted as she followed Rita into the foyer. Although the home was probably not much larger inside than Stella's townhome, she imagined it was easily over one million dollars.

"Let me show you around," Rita said, "and let her roam free."

Stella removed Jane's leash, and she started making her way around, sniffing here and there.

They walked through the kitchen, which had been renovated respectfully with period-specific fixtures, and then Rita led Stella through the living room and three small bedrooms. Rita had turned one of the bedrooms into a library. There was enough space for two overstuffed chairs. The room smelled wonderful to both Stella and Jane. Rita had wineglasses and a tray of crackers spread out on an old chest she was using as a coffee table.

"I checked," Rita said when she saw Stella looking everything over. "The wine and crackers are vegan."

"I'm ready to dig in," Stella said, sinking into one of the chairs.

Rita brought several boxes next to Stella's chair and sat in the other chair.

In between crackers and sips of her wine, Stella began to look through the books. There were several she could use for the Wild Librarian. She started sorting, putting ones she was not going to take in a separate pile off to the side.

"No," she said. "Definitely no way." She placed Henry Miller's *Crazy Cock* in the reject pile.

Rita laughed. "You might find another copy of that in there. At one point. I had about a dozen, just in case I came across people to give one to."

Stella was going through the largest box Rita had assembled when she called out, "Oh!" She had come across a beautiful copy of Barbara G. Walker's *The Woman's Dictionary of Symbols and Sacred Objects* from 1988. "I love this book," Stella said. "I used to have a copy that I misplaced somewhere along the way." She flipped through the book. "I may need to keep this for myself."

"Please do," Rita said. "I would be delighted." She was leaning back in her chair, balancing her wineglass against her round belly. Jane had curled up beside her.

Stella went back to sifting through the books. She pulled out a copy of Marija Gimbutas' *The Language of the Goddess*. Rita jerked forward, almost spilling her wine.

"How did that get in there?"

Stella handed the book to Rita. "Is this the copy you took to Big Sur?" she asked.

"It is I'm glad you found it and I didn't mistakenly take this box to the Goodwill." Rita opened to a page that had been turned down. "There it is," she said to Stella.

Stella moved closer to see better. It was the double goddess image from Rita's pilgrimage.

Before leaving, they stepped out into Rita's back yard. Jane ran around and howled as if she were in paradise. Rita lit a cigarette.

"Oh, I long for something like this," Stella said. Rita's back yard was over twice the size of what she had at her townhome. Beyond a grassy area, Rita had a rose garden. In another area, there was a picnic table surrounded by mature fruit trees.

"Obviously," Rita said, "it was well-established before I moved in, but I've added some things." She pointed to a blooming flower garden. Even from a good distance, Stella could see it was an attraction for bees. She breathed in all the scents.

"Do you think you'll be able to have something like this in the future?" Rita asked.

"I wouldn't have thought so just a few years ago, but it's becoming more possible. I imagined I would be living on less once I opened the bakery. That was true for a while. Over the past two years, I've turned a corner."

"Wonderful."

The sun was beginning to set.

"Come on, girl!" Stella laughed while calling out to Jane. "We need to load up some boxes and drive back to reality."

Near Rita's front door, as she got ready to carry the last box to the car, she looked closer at several framed photographs arranged over a small, elegant table. On the table was a vase with roses. Several candles had been arranged there with a brass incense burner. Stella realized she was possibly looking at something like an altar. She set the box down on the floor and studied one photograph that showed an attractive man sitting on a desk in front of an old-style chalkboard. His legs hung over the front. He appeared confident and at ease.

"That's Carl," Rita said. "That was his first year of teaching at the university—of course, many, many years before I met him. He was made for the job."

Stella began looking at the other photographs. One showed what she knew was a much older Carl in a tuxedo. Rita was next to him in the photograph wearing a gorgeous rose gown.

"What were you doing here?" Stella asked.

"Believe it or not, Carl's brother is a successful screenwriter. We were at the Academy Awards."

"Oh my God!"

"I know! It was shortly after we married."

As Stella took in the other photos, she realized the deep love Rita had for Carl. She knew she had carelessly minimized it in her mind considering he was Rita's fourth husband, but in this moment, seeing the roses, candles, incense burner, and photographs that illustrated various parts of his life story leading up to his marriage with Rita, she began to understand the depth of her loss.

"Let me ask you," Rita began.

Stella thought she heard a slight quiver in her voice, so she turned and caught her eye. Rita took in a deep breath, making a soft motion toward the photographs.

"Do you think it will happen for me again?"

Stella looked intently at Rita, feeling the importance of the question. The remaining sun in the early evening sky was causing a reflection to come through a small glass pane in the door. Stella remembered the crystal ball hanging just outside.

"I'm certain, Rita," she said. "Without a doubt."

Stella was right. It wasn't too long before John King appeared.

Rita first saw John King at the bakery's bicycle tune-up event held every spring. Taking place over a weekend in April, it started early on Saturday morning and went through Sunday afternoon. Several large pop-up canopies had been set up in a lot off the Wild Librarian's back patio. People from a local bicycle collective provided tune-ups, various small repairs, and tips for donations split evenly between the bakery and the collective.

Stella always loved the tune-ups and the new energy it brought to the bakery. Even if she had the day off, she would drop in for long stretches. She was talking to some young women from the collective when Rita appeared wearing her hot pink dress.

"Just stopping by for my rose pistachio," she told Stella as she glided by. Then she abruptly stopped and put her hand on Stella's forearm. "Ooh la la!" she let out, dropping her tongue out of her mouth to accent what she was expressing. She pointed, saying, "Look!"

Stella turned in the direction of Rita's finger. There was a man using a rag to wipe down a dusty bike.

"And who is that?" Rita asked.

"I don't know," Stella told her. "I suppose someone with the collective."

Rita walked over and started talking to the man. Stella couldn't help but look over from time to time. Rita would laugh and toss her hair around. She gestured wildly as she spoke, making her jeweled hands more noticeable. Within a few minutes, Rita had pulled the man away from his work and the two were gathered at a table eating rose pistachio cupcakes while sipping cappuccinos. They already had a relaxed and familiar togetherness. Rita would later tell Stella that while first talking to John, she felt and heard the even beat within her body.

"The tempo returned when I stood next to him," she told her. "The Big Sur sensation. It must have been my body getting ready. I felt that beat the whole way down to between my legs and even further into my toes. My, my."

Stella laughed.

"And do you know what I was getting ready for?" Rita asked.

"I'm sure I do," Stella said.

Rita tilted her head up and paused for a few seconds, the way she sometimes did to build suspense. She twirled her arms together in front of her like two snakes. "Stella," she began, "I was getting ready for . . . my sexual revolution." She took a bite of her cupcake.

"You!" Stella laughed. "I think your revolution happened a long time ago, old girl."

"No, I had never been with such an athlete. Let me share that it's different when you're with a man in his fifties who is still doing the California Double."

"The California Double?" Stella laughed. "I'm afraid to ask."

"You've never heard of it?" Rita said. "Oh, it's nothing dirty! It's when you surf and ski on the same day."

Stella smiled. "That's wonderful! Wow, John is certainly quite the athlete."

"He is," Rita told her, turning her body around in a little dance. "My man is an outdoor enthusiast." She couldn't help sharing another detail. "And just so you know, this man has an amazing appetite. He's not a California Double in bed. It's more of a quadruple."

Rita and John were a couple in no time. For all the happiness she'd had with Carl and the despair she initially felt over his passing, Rita was still able to fully enjoy herself with John. And John became a regular member of the Wild Librarian community, sometimes making it a destination after a long morning bicycle ride on the nearby trail that led to the ocean. Rita and John enjoyed many dinners with Andy and Alex, the Two A's, at Luna's Italian Restaurant next door before dropping into the bakery for dessert and extended conversation.

Considering Rita's marriage history, Stella wondered if the next one was on the horizon. One day, she mentioned this to Grace.

"How do you convince a man to be number five?" Grace asked Stella while arranging an order of Coconut Jazz Muffins in a bakery box. They had just received new custom sky-blue boxes.

Stella watched Grace close the lid and tie a thin purple ribbon around the box. "I would have no idea," she said, "but if anyone can do it, Rita surely can." In her mind, she saw flashes of Rita—the wind-chime baubles, her jeweled hands, her extravagant scarves, her large breasts, her dark tousled hair, and her hands making the shape of the double goddess in the air. She imagined the green van driving to Big

Sur, the chocolate donuts, and the peanut butter.

It was the morning of New Year's Eve when Stella saw Rita and John locking their bicycles on a rack across the street from the Wild Librarian. In the way holidays often hold anticipation, there was a soft electricity in the air. Stella didn't know Rita had started riding or even owned a bike. It seemed so unlike her. She was even wearing a sweat suit. Had she stopped smoking too? In the distance when she removed her bike helmet, Stella noticed how Rita's raven hair caught auburn highlights in the sun.

John got close to Rita and helped her adjust her backpack. It was a large pack. Stella thought there was probably a book or two inside. When Rita raised her hands to touch the straps, Stella smiled to see her overly jeweled hands.

That's definitely still Rita. She giggled to herself. *Just on a bike and in a sweat suit.*

When they got close to the bakery entrance, Stella could see Rita's face was sweaty.

"Chair! Chair, please!" Rita sat at the community table. She grabbed a water bottle from John's hand and took a good chug. "Oh boy!" she said to Stella, licking her lips. "We just rode here from John's place by the ocean."

"That must be at least fifteen miles!" Stella said, shocked and amused by what she was witnessing.

"She's a superstar," John said.

"It was John's idea," Rita explained, "to add something even more special to the day. We've come here to tell you important news and ask for a favor." Rita fanned herself for a few seconds with a newspaper someone had left at the table. She then did her head tilt to add to the suspense.

Stella waited.

"John proposed this morning. We want to get married this March. And we want to have our small wedding here."

Stella clapped and cheered, jumping up to hug Rita. "They're getting married!" she yelled. This made Grace and Andy run over.

Other customers applauded. The old couple the McDaniels were sitting in the overstuffed reading chairs. Eleanor McDaniels tapped her wooden walking stick loudly against the floor, causing vibrations beneath everyone's feet.

In the midst of the activity and loud celebrating, Stella looked at John. He was beaming. John clearly had no issue being number five.

Stella didn't have any experience with hosting a wedding, but she imagined Andy's expert handling of other events for the Wild Librarian could be put to good use. She also recalled Clare Fortune, who provided art workshops at the bakery, used to work as a wedding planner.

Clare and Andy ended up being a star team who pulled everything together in a short amount of time. Before long, the selected date of March 20 was upon them. In her mind, Stella saw the elaborate tiered display of Rose Pistachio Desire Cupcakes she would make. She also offered Rita an idea for music at the reception.

"Accordion music!" Rita looked startled, but she considered the idea. "That certainly would make it something to remember."

"I know the perfect person," Stella said.

Rita's eyes glowed and widened, but then something like panic crossed her face. "Wait a minute, Stella! You don't mean that poor tattered man who comes in here sometimes schlepping his old accordion with him."

"Oh, I do." Stella smiled. "That's exactly who I'm thinking of."

"With the clunky cowboy boots?"

"Well, they are actually engineer boots. He worked for a time for the railroad, so I think there is some pride and history there."

Rita leaned in and whispered, "But isn't he homeless?"

"I don't see what that has to do with it," Stella said, showing her disapproval.

Rita didn't budge, waiting.

"He was without a home when he first arrived several years ago.

As far as I know, he now rents a room here in the city," Stella told her.

"Uh-huh," Rita said slowly, looking in disbelief at Stella.

"Trust me on this one, Rita." Stella smiled. "I don't believe you'll be disappointed."

Rita decided to have faith in Stella. Guy Mandal, the self-described "traveling musician," was booked. Because of John and Rita's considerable budget, it was his best-paying gig, allowing him to pay several months in advance at the residential hotel where he lived in a small room.

The wedding reception was held inside the bakery, but the ceremony took place around the back of the building and under the pop-up canopies that came out every spring for the bicycle tune-up weekends. "It's like a full circle," Grace said. Several of Rita's colleagues from the university library were part of the small gathering of thirty. John's elderly parents drove up from San Diego, and Rita's younger brother and his wife flew in from Portland.

"My brother's a champ," Rita told Stella when they had a moment together during the reception, "because he's been at all five now."

Stella laughed. "Nothing like a good brother," she said, thinking of her Ben who provided encouragement even from a distance. "And what do you think of Guy Mandal's music?" She winked.

"Yes, yes." Rita laughed. "As always, you were right."

Stella giggled and clapped her hands together.

"All right, Stella." Rita smiled. "You were more than right. It's exquisitely romantic."

This moment with Rita allowed Stella to closely take in her dress. It was a Renaissance-style gown in soft lilac velvet with tiny white embroidered rosebuds on the bodice and sleeves. Although more tame than usual, her hair still had random wisps falling around her face. She wore a wreath made of white ribbons and pink roses, with tiny metallic stars and orbs bobbing here and there. Stella thought of the forest wreath Rita spontaneously made during her pilgrimage. Earlier, during the ceremony in the lot under the canopies, Rita had been barefoot, but now, she was wearing velvet slippers that matched her dress.

"Let's escape to my office for a moment," Stella said.

Once inside, Stella handed Rita a sky-blue bakery box. "This is for your eyes only," she said. "And John too."

Rita opened the box to find four cupcakes with different colored frostings The frosting was gathered in large dollops. She peered more into the box and lifted one out. As it came into the light, so did an uproarious laugh from both of them.

"Holy shit, Stella! Is this what I think it is?"

"You got it! I don't have the shape entirely right, but that's what you asked me for way back. You're holding the first and likely last batch of my Crazy Cock Cupcakes."

"Oh they smell divine."

"You're smelling the gorgeous strawberries from the farmers' market."

"Yum!"

"Scandalous strawberry cupcakes!" Stella then picked up a small box from her desk.

"And what do we have here?"

Stella opened the lid and tilted the box for Rita to see. Inside was a cupcake with a design drawn in thin lines of chocolate sauce. Rita immediately recognized the shape of the double goddess. She moved toward Stella and pulled her into her arms.

"Oh, my friend!" Rita said.

"That one is especially for you, pilgrim," Stella whispered into Rita's hair. "Chocolate and peanut butter."

Scandalous Strawberry Cupcakes
Recipe for approximately 24 regular-size cupcakes

1 1/2 cups strawberry puree
3 cups unbleached organic flour
1 cup organic raw sugar
2 teaspoons baking soda
1 teaspoon salt
3/4 cup organic oil
1/2 cup almond or macadamia nut milk
2 teaspoons vanilla
3/4 cup organic applesauce

Preheat oven to 350 degrees. Use a blender, fork, or other utensil to make your strawberry puree. (To get 1 1/2 cups of a puree, you will likely need about 3 cups of sliced strawberries. You can use frozen strawberries if you let them thaw first. If you plan to add strawberry frosting to your cupcakes, add about 1/2 cup extra strawberries when making your puree and save 3 tablespoons of the puree for the frosting.) In a separate large bowl, combine all the dry ingredients. By hand or with a handheld mixer, combine the applesauce, strawberry puree, oil, milk, and vanilla into the dry ingredients. The batter should be well-mixed and not lumpy. Pour batter into your baking cups. Ready to bake! Yay! Bake for 15–18 minutes. To make sure the cupcakes are ready, insert a toothpick near the center of one. If the toothpick comes out clean, you know they are done! If any batter sticks to the toothpick, they need to bake for longer. When cool, top with strawberry frosting.

Strawberry Frosting

Use an electric mixer to combine 3 cups organic powdered sugar with 2 tablespoons softened vegan butter. Once thick and well-combined, add three tablespoons of strawberry puree and 1/4 teaspoon organic vanilla extract. Keep mixing until it is the thickness you desire.

PERFECT PAIRING: Mmm . . . something erotic and sensual is recommended here. Why not read a passage from one of Anais Nin's diaries? Better yet . . . get yourself curled up in your favorite comfy chair and eat your cupcake while someone reads to you!

Rose Pistachio Desire Cupcakes
Recipe for approximately 12 regular-size cupcakes

1 1/4 cup unbleached organic flour
1/2 teaspoon organic vanilla extract
3/4 cup organic raw sugar
1/2 to 1 teaspoon rose water*
3/4 cup pistachios, finely ground
1/2 cup vegan butter, very soft
1/4 teaspoon salt
1 cup almond milk
2 teaspoons baking powder
1 tablespoon apple cider vinegar

Preheat oven to 350 degrees. In a large bowl, mix together all the dry ingredients, including the finely ground pistachios. You may want to sift the ingredients. To grind the pistachios, you can use a coffee grinder or other device. It's okay if some pieces are not finely ground. When mixing, try to eliminate any clumping of the ingredients. In a separate small bowl, combine the milk with the apple cider vinegar. Then add the vanilla extract and rose water. Add the wet ingredients to the dry ingredients and mix well. You should be able to easily pour the batter into your baking cups. Bake for 18–22 minutes. To make sure the cupcakes are ready, insert a toothpick near the center of one. If the toothpick comes out clean, you know they are done! If any batter sticks to the toothpick, they need to bake for longer. Once the cupcakes are cool, top with vanilla frosting. (See the Enchanted Lemon Pecan Cupcakes for a vanilla frosting recipe). For decoration and extra deliciousness, sprinkle the top with chopped or ground pistachios.

*Rose water can easily overpower a recipe, so be careful not to use too much. If baking with rose water is new for you, you may use 1/2 teaspoon the first time you make the cupcakes and adjust the amount you use the next time.

PERFECT PAIRING: Pick up a copy of *Directed by Desire*, June Jordan's collected poems, to read along with your desire cupcake. Warning: The fire and truth in June's poems may make you want to go out and change the world. (This is a good thing!)

Visions

No one could say why Tom Donald showed up to the vision board series in late spring one year. When Clare Fortune, the workshop leader, asked everyone to share a bit about themselves, Tom moved uncomfortably in his chair and remained silent. She didn't push.

Stella made a brief appearance with a tray of macaroons and smiled to herself after spotting Tom in his standard overalls and work shoes along with a dozen women of varying ages. She felt a sweetness toward him. He appeared to be in his seventies and had shared little about his life since he became a regular at the bakery last year.

Robert's wife Maria had left him a few years before Tom first showed up. Stella was hoping the two men would form a friendship since they were around the same age and often came to the bakery in the mornings within a few minutes of each other, but it was a stretch to even call them acquaintances. Sometimes, they shared a nod of acknowledgment. On more than one occasion, when the morning rush was over, Tom and Robert had remained sitting in the bakery, always with several tables in between them, both men lost in their thoughts or their newspapers. Their only connection seemed to be the solace the bakery offered them.

Stella knew Tom lived nearby in the large senior apartment

complex. Once, he came in with a younger woman he introduced as his daughter who was visiting from out of state. His daughter was lovely with Stella and Grace, talking easily about her own love of baking and reading and how she didn't have much time for these pleasures with her current work schedule. She told them about moving to Austin, Texas, and being surprised by how much she loved it. They learned a lot about her effortlessly and in a short time, but with her father, Stella noticed a formality, as if they didn't quite connect. Before Tom's daughter left that day, she purchased several books Stella recommended. When Tom came in alone two days later and ordered his coffee, Stella commented on how much she'd enjoyed talking to her.

"She's gone back," he told her. "Back to her life." He signaled he didn't want to talk by looking down, shuffling his newspaper, and opening it to the local news section. He made a grunt as if he were getting his body settled.

Tom only bought black coffee during his visits, and just once he purchased a book from the Wild Librarian: Thomas Moore's *The Re-enchantment of Everyday Life*. Stella found this odd but was delighted since this was one of her favorite books. She decided to try to approach Tom again one morning. She walked over with a Magical Day Muffin in a take-out box.

"Do you like cherries, blueberries, and peaches?" she asked.

"I do," Tom said. He had his copy of the Moore book with him. Stella noticed the corners of several pages were folded down. He had a pen clipped to the front pocket of his overalls. She wondered if he was making notes or underlining the text.

"On the house," Stella told him.

Tom looked up at Stella, taking the box and placing it on the table next to his coffee. "Thank you. I will try it."

"Are you enjoying it?" Stella asked him, making a gesture toward the book.

"I suppose I am," he said. "Mostly reading it to pass the time." He moved around a bit in his chair.

Stella sensed he was growing uncomfortable.

"Thank you for your generosity," he said to Stella, tapping the top of the box before moving his attention back to his book. As she turned to walk away, he surprised her by adding, "You've made a great place here."

During the first vision board session with Tom in attendance, Clare gave the participants an overview of her thoughts on artmaking. This included, "We are all artists;" "We create from the soul;" and, "We can heal our wounds with the creative spirit." She announced she would start each of the three sessions in the series with a question and they would have ninety minutes to create their piece, leaving thirty minutes for sharing. "No one is required to share," she explained, "unless you feel called to do so." She tried not to glance in Tom's direction when she said this.

Clare wore a flowing fuchsia tunic that complemented her mahogany complexion. Her dark hair was grouped together in the back with a sequined barrette. Tom was attentive as he sat with his legs stretched out and his hands in the side pockets of his overalls, but he gave no indication of approval or dismissal of Clare's proclamations on art. The three women who shared his table gave him sideways glances. He added a touch of apprehension but also extra wonderment to the day.

"Okay, everyone," Clare said with her hands in front of her as if in prayer, "I'm going to reveal today's question: Where do you feel the most at peace?" She paused for several seconds and repeated the question. "All right!" She clapped her hands together twice. "Let's get started."

Clare provided each of the women and Tom with scissors and an artboard, instructing them to share the supplies on the table to create their vision board related to the question. There were a dozen or so magazines, markers, glue, glitter, and colored pencils.

As they started working, jazz came on over the bakery's sound system. No one required further explanation. Within minutes, the Wild

Librarian was filled with the sound of scissors cutting, fingers tearing paper, and women's voices with occasional laughter. Everyone, including Tom, worked hunched slightly forward over the tables.

A song came on that made Tom pause. He stopped working on his board and closed his eyes. None of the women at his table noticed since they were immersed in their artmaking, but Clare happened to look over and see him. Within the flurry of activity, his stillness was even more prominent. Clare realized she was being impolite and even intrusive by staring at him, but his peacefulness drew her in. Then she realized maybe she was reading this incorrectly and something could be wrong, so she walked over to his table. Not wanting to startle him, she let out a barely audible sigh when she got close and gently placed her hand on his right shoulder.

"Are you doing okay?" she asked him softly, trying not to draw attention.

"Yes," he said.

Clare knew then that nothing must have been wrong. She noticed some loose slivers of paper had fallen onto his work shoes and into his lap. He had used a blue pencil to color the perimeter of his artboard, and he was pasting white and pink circles he'd cut out from a magazine in the middle.

"Do you like the song?" she asked.

"I do, very much. It's Charles Mingus. 'Alice's Wonderland.'"

"Hmm. I don't know much about this type of music," Clare said.

"I know almost every song with 'Alice' in the title," Tom said.

"Why is that?"

"Alice was my wife's name."

Perhaps it was the meditative quality of the vision board exercise or the tranquility of the song descending over Tom that allowed him to share this personal information with Clare. Her intuition and Tom's silence leading up to this point told her it was a rare occurrence. She took it as a gift, nodded, and slowly made her rounds to the next table.

Tom didn't look up after mentioning his wife, so he was relieved when he heard Clare's voice several feet away commenting on someone's use of fruit images.

When time was running out, Clare gave everyone a ten-minute warning. 'Artists!" she said. "Your visions are beautifully manifesting. We are all in for a treat, I promise you!" She explained that as they finished, they should raise their hands. She would take each board to the other side of the bakery where two large tables had been pushed together in front of the art mural wall to display the creations. There would be a five-minute viewing of everyone's vision boards, followed by an optional sharing. Clare discouraged critique of others' works, rankings, or self-criticism.

The vision boards, collectively arranged, created an amazing burst of color. Some women couldn't refrain from making "ooh" and "ahh" sounds. Tom stood with the others, taking it all in.

Although everyone did their best to follow Clare's instructions and not rank or judge, Tom's creation stood out. It was well-executed and harmonious. It was subtle yet powerful. But it was more than that. His was undoubtedly the most magical and illusive. Clare knew this instantly when she was gathering the boards and picked up Tom's to place it near the center of the others. It was a part of the collective display yet also independent in its beauty and abstract nature. His use of layered shapes and colors gave the work a textured feel some of the others only lightly reached toward. Various round and circular shapes rushed out from the center of the board where they met cylinders of vibrant colors. Here and there were smaller shiny cutouts that shone like gems. Most of the other visions were full of specific images, such as women, animals, and flowers, along with words or phrases clipped from the magazines. Tom's offered nothing so direct. It was up to the viewer to determine the meaning, and the women had different unspoken responses to it.

One young woman couldn't help herself while she gazed at Tom's creation. Breaking the silence, she proclaimed, "Mind-blowing." Others whispered among themselves. What did it mean, they wondered, that Tom had created this in response to the question, "Where do you feel the most at peace?" Did this truly evoke peace for him? It certainly could, a few of them reasoned, but others wondered if he forgot the question.

When it came time to share, everyone returned to their seats with their boards. A few women eagerly stood one after the other to share what the vision board meant to them. Then the participation slowed. Clare waited, knowing some of the shyer women would start to come forward. A few did, but everyone was waiting to hear from Tom. Surely, he would tell them something and offer at least a clue.

Most were patient, scanning the others with their eyes to keep from looking in Tom's direction, but a few were not able to stop themselves from looking directly at him several times. Some women even felt angry, as if he were withholding information from them unfairly, although several of them, like Tom, did not share about their creations.

Clare could sense the distress growing. Starting to feel anxious herself, she asked, "Would anyone else like to share?"

It was quiet. The desire to look at Tom or call on him to speak bubbled up higher in the women, but Tom sat still in his chair in the same posture he'd had at the beginning of the workshop, with his legs stretched out and his hands in the pockets of his overalls. His masterpiece lay on the table, completely noncommittal, owing the others nothing.

Clare then thought he might be entirely oblivious to what was going on, and her heart softened. She let a few more seconds pass and then dismissed everyone. "Stay well," she told them. "Until we meet again."

The women appeared eagerly for the second session of the series. Everyone sat as before, as if there were assigned seats. The materials for artmaking were spread across the tables, and Clare already had the blank artboards ready to go in front of them.

Tom was noticeably absent when the time came to begin. Several women glanced at his empty chair. Even without him there, it was as if they could sense his presence.

At the last minute, as Clare was about to begin, he walked through the bakery door. Stella was near the entrance arranging new books in a display when he appeared. "Welcome, Tom," she said. He nodded and walked across the room to claim the empty seat.

"All right," Clare began, "I believe everyone made it back." She reminded them of the format and then asked the question, "What is your biggest dream?"

Everyone started busily working on their boards. Some followed Tom's lead from the first session and focused on colors and shapes instead of words and specific images. Clare noticed some of the women couldn't help but get up and walk around to pass by Tom's table and see what he was creating. Was the first time just a fluke?

It was clear by halfway in that Tom was creating another work of art. Clare peered over his shoulder from behind and delighted in what she saw developing. Then the collective display took place. Everyone gathered, taking in the rich creativity. Clare, trying not to center Tom's vision this time, placed his work over to the right side. This only caused the energy of all the creations to land there as if the others had been dimmed behind a bright light.

Tom's vision board was a collage of overlapping shapes that resembled mountains. They were rose and sapphire and cream-colored, laid over each other until they became like water. Small red fissures appeared here and there with slivers of glossy paper Tom had cut out from a magazine ad. Was it maybe the ocean and not the mountains? A few of them wondered about this. Or was it not even on earth, but in outer space or heaven? They were mesmerized.

A group of customers who were not part of the workshop also gathered around to take in the creations. One woman pointed out Tom's collage to her friend. "Look!" she said. They both gazed at the rose, sapphire, and cream with hints of red and gold. "Are these for sale?" the woman asked loudly to be heard above the clamor.

Clare walked over. "These are from our workshop tonight," she explained. "I suppose you would have to ask the artists."

Some women giggled. It was an exciting moment to think someone wanted to make a purchase. But of course, the woman was only interested in the one piece.

"This one," she said, pointing to Tom's. "Is this one for sale?"

It grew quiet. Clare and the workshop students all turned to where they knew Tom was standing on the opposite side of the table from his creation. He had his hands clasped in front of him instead of inside his pockets.

"Tom," Clare began, "it looks like you have a customer. Is your piece for sale?"

"I'm afraid it's not," Tom responded. It was the first time most of the women had heard his voice. Could this be the moment when they would discover more? Because everyone was looking at him, he spoke again. "I'm sorry. I'm afraid it's not for sale."

"Well," the woman said, "beautiful work. Truly wonderful." This caused one of the students to clap, which led to the others joining in until everyone was applauding.

Tom leaned forward in a slight bow to show his thanks. Clare had never experienced such a moment during her workshops. She felt a sense of elation, as if something mysterious was unfolding.

It took a longer moment of transition to get everyone back in their chairs and focused for the optional sharing. Clare waited, and then one woman raised her hand. She choked up and said her biggest dream was to find a partner. She held up her vision board: blended images of people together with flowers and trees. Another woman held up a board created in shades of blue with "peace" across the front. Several more shared, but again, the person everyone was waiting for remained silent. Still, the return to sharing created a welcome equilibrium. Clare asked everyone to start cleaning up and bring their two boards back for the final session next week, which they would conclude with a grand finale-style display.

Stella came around with a tray of lemon cookies. "A night cap," she told everyone. Passing by Tom, she noticed his creation on the table in front of him. Looking up, she caught Clare's eye from several tables over. "Wow," Stella mouthed. Clare gave a gentle nod back.

Tom reached up and took two cookies off the tray. He had nothing to say. That was how the night ended.

By the third session, most women had resigned themselves to the fact Tom would create something wonderful but they would not hear from him. It could have been the comradery they now felt as a group, or maybe it was because they were too excited to see what he created to care any longer about the fact he wouldn't speak, but most of the women were no longer angry at Tom. They had gotten into a rhythm together that included him, and even though he never shared, he was like the glue that held them together with a palpable suspense. Some women even felt something like love for him. His silence was no longer maddening, but a thing of wonder. The women at Tom's table couldn't help but feel a little more fortunate than the others. The tables were all close together, but they were still the chosen ones who got to sit with the mysterious silent man, the artist among the crowd. Their table brought forth divinity, which they believed might also have to do a little with them.

Clare wore one of her signature tunics. Several women commented on the rich burgundy shade of the linen. She stood up front by the mural wall where a few more tables with "reserved" signs had been arranged. Everyone, including Tom, was in their seats. Classical music played softly in the background.

"Welcome back, artists! Visioneers! As you can see, Stella has been kind to offer us several more tables. We will conclude tonight with a viewing of all your creations from our three weeks together. But first, it's time for your final vision." Clare paused, letting the suspense build. "What cherished memory from your life will you carry with you into the future?" she finally asked. "Let's create!"

Everyone got to work, and when the time was up and they gathered around for the grand finale viewing, there were long pauses to take in Tom's work. There was his first creation with its round shapes and cylinders, last week's mysterious landscape, and now, a final work that was even more stunning than the others. Tom had used one of the thick black pens to create an elegant line drawing of a woman surrounded by what looked like clouds and rocks. Lines extending outward from her torso bloomed into vines with vibrant purple flowers. The women leaned in to try to make out what was written near the bottom of the woman. Soon, there were various scattered comments.

"Alice."

"It says Alice."

"He wrote Alice."

"Alice."

Clare knew from her interaction with Tom the first week when the song "Alice's Wonderland" had played that this final vision was of his wife.

Stella was talking with Andy and Grace near the bakery case a few days after the vision board series ended when Tom came in for his morning coffee. Stella was interested in adopting a second dog through the rescue she'd adopted Jane from many years before. Jane was getting older and calmer, so she thought she could handle another older dog.

"How old is Jane now?" Andy asked.

"Already around eight. Can you believe it? I'm thinking a second dog a little younger or around her age would be good."

Tom reached the counter.

"Good morning, Tom," Andy greeted. "The usual?"

Tom nodded. He took his large coffee mug and made his way toward a table by the bookshelves. Stella noticed someone had left a dish at the table, so she quickly caught up with him.

"Let me clear that off for you, Tom."

He stood waiting, holding the newspaper and his copy of *The Re-enchantment of Everyday Life*, which was looking more tattered. Stella smiled to herself.

"I love dogs," Tom said. Stella was a bit surprised when he spoke.

"I can't have one where I live now."

"Not even a small one?" Stella asked.

"No," he said, taking his seat, "but I like big dogs anyway."

"Me too! I don't think you've met Jane yet—my German shepherd. I sometimes bring her with me to the back patio or slip her into my office if I'm just stopping in briefly."

Tom's eyes slightly widened, and Stella noticed a small, rare smile. "I didn't know," he told her. "I had one of those before. Charlie. A fine dog. He lived to be fifteen."

"They are the best dogs in my opinion," Stella told him.

Tom didn't respond. Was the conversation over?

"I'm thinking of getting another one," she told him.

"Another German shepherd?" he asked, starting to look at his newspaper.

"Yes, one to keep Jane company."

"Hmm," was all he said, putting his attention more on the paper.

Stella stepped away to straighten up the community table. She caught Andy and Grace watching in the distance and knew they must have been trying to listen in on the rare conversation. Andy raised his eyebrows.

It was a stretch to ask, but a few weeks later, when she had an appointment set to go to the German shepherd rescue kennel, Stella approached Tom. He was in one of his usual spots sipping on his morning coffee. Robert Gonzales was a few tables over at his window seat.

"Good morning, Robert. How are you doing today?"

"Doing well, Stella. Good morning." Robert returned to looking out the window, watching cars and people pass—something that seemed to still bring him some joy.

"Good morning, Tom," Stella called out as she walked toward him.

He looked up and nodded. "Good morning, Stella."

"I have a question for you."

Tom put his paper down. His expression shifted. Stella couldn't tell if he was intrigued, afraid, or just bothered.

"We talked about dogs recently."

"I remember."

"Well, the time has come. I'm going out to a kennel this weekend to meet some dogs."

"That sounds fine. German shepherds?"

"Yes."

Tom moved his feet around and adjusted his body in his chair. "Well, I hope you find a good one."

"I was thinking you might like to go with me. To meet the dogs."

"Me?" He was clearly puzzled. "Why?"

"I could use a second opinion, and it sounds like you have experience."

"You mean ride together?"

"Yes." Stella laughed. "We would probably have to do that."

"Where?"

"Near Laguna Beach. Shouldn't take us more than thirty minutes or so to get out there."

"I don't know."

"All right. You think about it."

Tom was already inside the Wild Librarian when Stella came by to pick him up. She walked across the bakery from the back entrance.

"Ready soon?" she asked. She saw he was finishing a Magical Day Muffin. She smiled to herself, assuming the one she gave him as a gift a little while back must have been a hit.

The drive to Laguna Beach was a breeze once they hit the freeway. Stella kept NPR on low, thinking the soft sounds might make Tom more comfortable. It was the regular weekend show in which someone was on the line trying to solve a word puzzle. She explained they would be meeting several dogs. Tom mostly offered a "yes" or "no" as Stella spoke.

They hit a stretch of traffic once they were on the canyon road, near the art college. Stella noticed Tom watching everything out the side window. They stopped at a light while groups of students passed by the front of the car going to different parts of the campus that spread out on both sides of the road.

"It's beautiful here, isn't it?" she asked.

"Yes, and expensive."

"That's true!" Stella laughed. She turned into a gravel lot that was up high and overlooked the ocean. When they opened the car doors they could hear dogs barking. "We're definitely here," she told Tom.

They walked toward the building that housed kennels around the back. Both Stella and Tom were wearing their construction boots, which Stella found amusing. Tom was in his overalls. He still had the pen clipped to his front pocket.

A woman who identified herself as Martha met them on the pathway before they reached the building. "Stella, right?"

"Yes. And this is my friend, Tom."

Martha nodded toward Tom. "You adopted . . . what was her name?" Martha asked. She had a hint of a southern drawl.

"Jane, but you called her Snowy."

"Right, right! It's been a long time. How is Jane doing?"

"She's great. Howls up a storm. She's in her early senior years, but you wouldn't know it."

"And you're a college professor?"

"You have a good memory! Yes, I used to be a librarian and I taught at the college. I left to open my own business a few years back."

"Really? That's quite a change. What is it?"

"The Wild Librarian Bakery and Bookstore."

"I'll be damned. I've heard of it. It's kind of famous, right?"

Stella laughed. "I'm fortunate it's been successful, but I don't know if it's famous."

Martha led them around back. The dogs were going wild barking and howling in their kennels. Stella looked at Tom. He was scanning the property with a large smile on his face. His shoulders were relaxed and his body less closed off. He almost seemed like a different person.

"You're looking for an older one, right?" Martha asked.

"Yes, at least age five."

Over the next hour, Stella and Tom met several dogs. Stella delighted in seeing Tom's excitement. It was near the end of their visit when Martha brought a curious-looking one out. He had white feet but a mostly black body with a brown face. He pranced toward them.

"This one we call Peanut," Martha said. "We think he's around seven and maybe a Dutch and German shepherd mix."

Although some of the dogs were understandably guarded, Peanut came right up. He licked Tom's hand and came over to Stella, sniffing her boots and jeans.

"You can pet this one without any worry," Martha said.

Stella touched his fur. It was thick, rough, and dry. He was clearly in need of a good bath. "What's his story?" she asked.

"We don't know much. He was found as a stray down in San Clemente. By his temperament, it's clear he's used to people. He gets along with most of the dogs here."

Tom was bending forward petting Peanut's head. Stella saw how he gently placed his old hands near Peanut's ears and then along his neck. She looked at the dog's soft brown eyes.

"Would you like to take him for a walk?" Martha asked.

Stella and Tom walked Peanut around the property. He was good on a leash. They took him down the street and came to an overhang where they could look out at the ocean. Stella breathed in the air and let out a sigh.

"I feel good about this one," she said.

"Me too. He kind of reminds me of Charlie." Stella recognized the name as Tom's old dog he mentioned to her at the bakery. "Peanut though," Tom said, clicking his tongue. "That's not a name for a majestic dog like this."

Stella laughed. "I was thinking the same thing. He would definitely need a new name!"

"Something more robust," Tom said, patting Peanut's side as if to demonstrate the dog's hardiness.

They walked Peanut back and made arrangements for the rescue to bring him to Stella's home to meet Jane the following weekend.

On the drive back to Santa Ana, Tom was more talkative than he had ever been with Stella or anyone at the bakery. It must have been the energy and excitement from being around the dogs. Stella decided to ask him about the vision board workshops.

"I saw the art you made during Clare's workshop," she began. "Really beautiful work, Tom."

"Thank you."

"You enjoyed it—the workshop?"

"I did." He took to looking out the side window.

They were on the canyon road again, passing by the art college. A group of young women carrying portfolios came onto the crosswalk.

"I studied art before," Tom said.

Stella was intrigued. "Really? You mean in college?"

"Yes. I started as an art major. Cal State Long Beach."

"What kind of art?"

"Mostly painting, oils, watercolors, but also some printmaking."

"That's wonderful."

"My dad got ill though, so I dropped out my junior year to help my mom take care of him. It was just us three and my older sister, who has since passed away."

"You didn't go back."

"No, got married. Had our daughter." He placed his hands on

his thighs, still looking out the window. "And I ended up working for close to forty years as a warehouse manager in Norwalk. Lighting equipment."

Stella asked him about his wife.

"Her name was Alice. She passed away many years ago now from ALS, or Lou Gehrig's disease."

"Oh, Tom."

"You know it?"

"A former colleague's husband passed away from ALS. I visited them several times and saw his tragic decline. I'm very sorry."

"Yeah." He tapped the fingers of his right hand on the car door below the window. "Don't know how I made it through that. My daughter dropped out of college to help me care for Alice. It was a stressful time that exhausted us. I fell into a terrible depression the last brutal months and became bitter. Once her mom passed away, my daughter returned to school and has pretty much stayed away ever since. I think she wanted to get as far away as she could."

They were silent for several minutes. Then Tom spoke again.

"I've made more art since the workshop."

"Since the workshop with Clare?"

"Yes."

"Wow, that's wonderful, Tom!"

"It surprises me. To be honest, it's almost all I do when I'm not running errands or coming into your place." He let out a small laugh.

"It's been many weeks since the workshop now, right? Have you created a lot?"

Tom laughed more. "Good Lord, yes. Probably close to fifty collages or, as Clare calls them, vision boards."

"I'd love to see them," Stella told him. They had reached Santa Ana, and she was making her way through the downtown streets to reach the bakery. The sky was gray and overcast, causing the purple blossoms on the jacaranda trees to contrast and pop. "Tom, why don't you come over when the rescue brings Peanut by next Saturday? You could bring your art." She waited through several seconds of silence.

"Sounds good," he said.

When they reached the Wild Librarian, Stella parked, and they both went inside. Rita Johansen was there with her new husband, John.

"It's the newlyweds," Stella said, greeting them with a hug.

"So . . .?" Andy came out from behind the bakery case. "Any prospects?"

"Prospects for what?" Rita asked.

"I'm thinking of adopting a second dog!"

"Fabulous," John said.

Stella got her phone out. "Let me show you."

They gathered around to see several photos of Peanut.

"What a beauty!" Andy said.

"So handsome," Rita chimed in. "What's his name?"

"Well, the rescue names them, but I could change his name."

"So . . .?" Rita asked again.

"They're calling him Peanut."

Everyone laughed, including Tom who was standing off slightly by the bookshelves.

"Tom says he will need a more robust name," Stella said.

"Oh!" Rita's face lit up. "Let me see him again." She studied the image on Stella's phone. "Yes! Yes! Don't you know?" Stella and everyone waited. "He looks like a Henry!"

Everyone except Tom laughed since he did not understand the joke.

"Rita has an obsession with the writer Henry Miller," Stella explained.

"I think she's right," Tom said. "Henry would be a fine name for him."

Rita winked at Stella.

Stella saw Tom walking up the pathway to her townhome a few minutes before eleven the following Saturday morning. He was carrying a handsome large tan portfolio under his right arm that closed with a thick black ribbon. Tom stopped to admire the small garden Stella had cultivated in the front. Bees were buzzing in tall lavender bushes that surrounded a trail of stepping-stones.

"Tom, welcome!" Stella called out, opening the door.

Jane came running down the stairs and howling as she took her customary position next to Stella.

"Oh my," Tom said, seeing Jane for the first time. "I wasn't expecting the white fur."

"She's stunning, isn't she?"

Jane looked up at Tom with her large brown eyes accented by tiny white eyelashes.

"And a German shepherd?"

"Yes, but because of that howl, I wonder if there isn't some husky or wolf mixed in." Stella smiled.

Tom came in and sat on Stella's overstuffed sofa. He leaned his portfolio against the coffee table. "It smells good in here," he said. "Almost like the bakery."

"I've heard that before." Stella laughed. "I just took some banana spice muffins out of the oven."

"I think I smell cinnamon."

"Yes, it's a new recipe with spices from Riviera's, the shop next to the bakery. I'm thinking of calling them Walt's Banana Spice Muffins for Walt Whitman." Once she said it, she was thankful Tom didn't ask why. She didn't want to mention how the bread was sensual and earthy like Whitman's poetry, thinking such details could make Tom uncomfortable.

Jane jumped up next to him on the sofa, knocking over a pillow, and Stella made a gesture to get her down.

"I don't mind," Tom said. "I rather like it."

Jane gave the side of his face a large lick, making them both laugh as he wiped his face with the sleeve of his shirt.

"That's a sharp-looking portfolio," Stella said, nodding toward where Tom rested it.

"It's actually quite old. The 1970s to be exact."

"From art school?"

"Yes, I managed to keep it all these years. Stuff made back then lasts."

The doorbell rang. Martha had already arrived with Peanut. Stella was to bring Jane out, and they would practice walking the dogs on the sidewalk at a good distance apart.

"Let's go down to the end and back," Martha said, pointing and moving toward the sidewalk. Her southern drawl was more pronounced as she gave directions. There was a young man with her from the rescue who identified himself as Aaron.

Tom, Stella, and Jane followed Peanut, Martha, and Aaron. The dogs were more concerned with sniffing the plants and grass along the sidewalk than bothering with each other.

"This is positive," Martha said, marching forward with Peanut.

They made their way to the end of the block and turned back toward Stella's. The dogs got closer together, doing a little sniffing.

"Since it's going well," Martha commented, "why don't we take them to your back yard, but keep them on their leashes?"

They all walked through Stella's to the outside where she had a small yard and patio area. It was surrounded by a tall stucco wall on all sides covered in blooming bougainvillea.

"The size isn't ideal for two big dogs," Martha said, "but it will do."

Stella didn't realize she was also being evaluated still.

They all sat at her large patio table. Within a few minutes, both dogs lay down.

"Well, well," Martha said, "this is one of the best meet-and-greets we've had in a long time."

Stella looked at Aaron. He was busy scrolling on his phone.

"Why don't we let them interact off their leashes?" Tom suggested.

After some hesitation, Martha agreed.

Jane let out a few howls once her leash was removed. She ran around the small space and got down to rub her back against the grass. Her white paws flew around in the air as she snorted. Peanut got close and barked, but this only made Jane roll around more. Then she got up and they took off, making a few laps together and passing by the table with each go-around. A few growls from Jane made Stella's stomach jumpy, but it became clear it was all about play.

The meet-and-greet ended with Stella making the decision to adopt.

"Great! We'll get the paperwork all ready and bring him back in a few days. How is Wednesday?"

"Perfect," Stella said. "Oh, and by the way, I'll be naming him Henry."

Once Martha, Aaron, and Henry left, Stella went inside with Tom. She motioned toward the kitchen table. "Tom, why don't you bring your portfolio over here? We can spread it out." She brought over two plates with a large banana muffin on each.

Jane took her customary post under the table, where she sat whenever food was being served.

Tom opened his portfolio and began to lay out his art, which was mostly abstract collages. Stella was stunned by the richness and harmony in each piece, but together, they created a body of work that was clearly by the same skilled hand. She noted the three he'd made in Clare's workshop within the collection.

"Tom," Stella began, "I'm truly speechless." She placed her hand over her heart. "These are beautiful."

Tom encouraged her to leaf through the pile of several dozen.

She pulled out the ones she wanted to know more about.

"May I ask about this one?" she said, pointing to a collage composed of mostly creams and beige tones, yet a jagged black line, possibly made by acrylic paint, appeared here and there. Although it was mostly calming, Stella found the jagged line unsettling and ambiguous.

"Following the workshop," he told Stella, "I made contact with Clare."

"Yes."

"She gave me dozens of questions I could use to create more visions."

"How wonderful. Do you recall the question for this one?"

"Yes. 'What is a great sorrow you survived?'"

Stella waited to hear more.

"This is about when my wife, Alice, lost her voice. From the ALS. The last year, she could not speak. I longed for her voice, for her to be able to say anything. Our home became quiet. From that point on, she declined. Within that silence, there was a dread."

Stella's eyes continued to scan the piece as he spoke. She felt honored by Tom's willingness to share. Next, she selected a collage with gray vertical lines. It was an orderly piece. Tom had written numbers in the center and around the edges. Within the lines, he'd glued various small pieces of paper to appear as objects on shelves. It was strikingly different to the previous one about Alice's silence. Something about the organization was pleasing to Stella.

"That is my old warehouse where I worked all those years."

"Oh, yes, I can see that now."

"The question was, "Where have you spent too much of your time?'"

"Hmm," Stella replied, feeling the weight of the question and his artistic response. She continued to look through the creations, asking Tom to comment on different ones. "Has Clare seen these?" she asked.

"Oh, no. You're the first person."

"They are so wonderful, Tom. They speak to me. Such soulful work."

"Thank you."

Stella was beginning to see more into Tom's life and personality. She could sense he was pleased. He sat down to begin eating the banana muffin, so Stella did the same.

"At the bakery, as I'm sure you know, we've had some art shows using portable display walls. We set them up temporarily in front of the wall with the art mural." She looked at Tom and was surprised to find him watching her intently and listening. *He knows where I'm going with this, and he's going to say yes*, Stella thought, feeling her heart leap. "What do you say, Tom? Are you ready for your first solo show?"

He only paused for a few seconds. "I'll do it," he said.

Jane came over to him as if she could sense something good had just happened. He rubbed the sides of her big head while she let out one of her dog snorts.

They finished eating the bread while talking about possibilities. Stella looked up the bakery's calendar on her phone. They selected the month of May. "I'll hire Clare to help you get everything ready," she told him.

Tom pulled on the ribbon wrapped around his portfolio. Stella could sense a bit of reservation beginning to build in the way he was holding his shoulders and touching the ribbon. She thought he was likely questioning his quick response, but she could also feel excitement around him. He began to gather his art to place it back in the portfolio.

"I almost forgot." He turned to Stella with one of the collages in his hands. "You didn't ask about this one." He was smiling.

Stella looked. It was a collage with a blue background. Tiny rectangular objects, possibly books, floated around the space. They were in various colors but mostly golds, reds, and deeper blues than the background. A few must have been cut from a catalog or magazine since they had random text on them. Stella experienced the piece as being full of joy, airiness, and exuberance.

"I love it!" Stella told him. "Are these books?"

"Yes, and do you see this?" He pointed to different places. "The swirls."

"I do, like steam."

"Exactly! Like steam from a coffee cup."

Stella was captivated by the piece. She turned it in different directions.

"The question for this one was, 'Where do you like to spend your mornings?'" Tom explained.

"No!" Stella exclaimed, making Jane sit up again and howl. "Is it what I think?"

"It is. It's the Wild Librarian!"

Clare Fortune advertised Tom's art opening through her business, and Stella did the same through the bakery. The show was featured as something to do in the *LA Weekly*, and it was included in the arts calendar of the *Los Angeles Times*.

The space couldn't hold all of Tom's work that deserved to be shown, but it had room for the forty pieces Clare curated. Tom wanted to title the show "Alice" after his wife. Clare encouraged him to go with other titles since only a few of his creations were specific to Alice or their marriage. "No, you don't understand," he told her. "Everything is about Alice." Clare remembered how she'd stepped back from pushing Tom to speak during the workshops. He was so resolute in his conviction something told her to not push here either, so the show was titled "Alice."

The bakery was full of an electric energy the day Clare, Tom, and the Two A's worked together to finalize the exhibit. Tom's visions mysteriously glowed under the bakery's lights. Instead of titles, the questions Clare had given Tom were typed beneath each vision. The one Stella knew was a vision of the Wild Librarian was part of the show.

A few minutes before the official opening, Clare wrapped her body in her arms as she stood next to Stella taking in the exhibit. "They are pulsating. So alive," Clare said.

"I feel it too." Stella smiled.

The surprise of the night was when Tom's daughter appeared. Tom said he had invited her, but she didn't know if she would be able to get away to fly to California. Stella and Grace immediately recognized her as she stood near the entrance scanning the crowded room. They offered to bring her to Tom who was doing his best, as a man used to expressing very little, to talk to a group of admirers who had gathered around him, including several women who were part of the vision board workshop series. As they made their way zigzagging around people, Stella was surprised to see Robert Gonzales in the crowd. She couldn't recall the last time she'd seen him at the Wild Librarian in the evening or at an event. He was dressed in an impeccable navy suit with a patterned tie.

Tom turned and saw his daughter when she was a few steps away. He was unable to contain the joy in his face.

"Dad," his daughter said, looking from him to his art, "I had no idea."

Tom and his daughter huddled close together, sharing a brief conversation no one else could hear. Stella and Grace watched Tom's daughter put her arms around her father, bending forward slightly and resting her head against his chest.

"I think you've outdone yourself this time," Grace whispered to Stella while handing her a glass of champagne.

"It's certainly magical," she said, taking a sip.

"Did you see Robert is here?"

"I did! It looks like he's wearing a new suit."

"I spoke to him when he first arrived," Grace said. "I noticed the suit too. I complimented him."

"It's so good to see him out like this," Stella said. There were a few cheers and applause from a small group gathered around Tom and his daughter.

"Maybe he's feeling better from the swimming classes," Grace offered.

"Swimming classes? He's returned?" Stella remembered how swimming was a big part of Robert's life before his wife Maria left.

"Yes. I overheard him tell Andy the other morning. He started up last week."

Stella felt her heart lift. She looked around and found Robert viewing the exhibit. He was holding a plate with a thick slice of Poet's Beer Bread.

"You know, Grace," Stella said with a large smile, "tonight is much more than magical. It's stupendous, fabulous, extraordinary, and . . . it's . . . another word I can't think of at the moment."

Grace laughed, and Stella took another sip of her champagne before walking to the back to bring out more trays of freshly baked muffins and cupcakes.

Tom's exhibit remained up for two months, bringing dozens of people to the Wild Librarian for the first time each week. Several days after the exhibit was taken down, Andy came to Stella's office in the afternoon.

"While you were out, Tom stopped by," he said, holding what appeared to be a large thin box. "He left this for you."

"I didn't know he was coming by. He couldn't stay?" Stella moved some invoices for book orders to her chair to make room for the box on her desk.

"No, remember," Andy said, "today is the big day? He was on his way to the airport to go visit his daughter."

"Oh, that's right! His Austin trip."

Andy left Stella alone in her office. She could hear him talking with customers. He was playing his favorite classic rock station, and Jackson Browne's "Your Bright Baby Blues" came on. It was a song Stella liked. She hummed along as she began to remove the thick paper wrapped around the box. Pulling off the lid, she found Tom's abstract, stunning vision of the Wild Librarian inside, beautifully framed.

Stella lifted it, wondering if she should hang this personal and enchanting creation at home or at the bakery when an envelope attached to the back fell to the floor. She placed the art down and reached for it, finding a small white note card inside. It read, "For Stella. You make things happen. —Tom."

Magical Day Muffins
Recipe for 12 regular-size or 6 jumbo muffins

1 1/2 cups unbleached organic flour
3/4 cup organic almond or
1/2 cup organic raw sugar
macadamia nut milk
2 teaspoons baking powder
1/4 cup organic oil
1 teaspoon salt
3/4 cup assorted and chopped
1/2 teaspoon cinnamon
frozen fruit, including cherries, peaches, and blueberries
1/4 teaspoon ginger
a little extra organic raw sugar

Preheat oven to 400 degrees. Mix dry ingredients together first. Add milk and oil. Fold in the frozen fruit that you've chopped into small pieces. Batter will be lumpy. Use a spoon to put batter into your baking cups. Sprinkle a little of the extra raw sugar on top before putting them in the oven. Bake for 18–24 minutes. To make sure the muffins are ready, insert a toothpick near the center of one. If the toothpick comes out clean, you know they are done! If any batter sticks to the toothpick, they need to bake for longer.

PERFECT PAIRING: Mary Oliver's poems celebrate the beauty and magic of nature and elevate our common everyday experiences into a wondrous realm. Stella recommends some of her favorite Oliver poems to enjoy with these muffins: "Wild Geese," "The Summer Day," and "When I am Among the Trees."

Walt's Banana Spice Muffins
Recipe for approximately 12 regular-size muffins

3 ripe bananas
¼ cup organic oil
1 cup organic raw sugar
2 cups unbleached organic flour
1 teaspoon salt
1 teaspoon cinnamon
½ teaspoon ginger
dash of cloves
1 teaspoon baking soda
small amount of organic raw sugar to sprinkle on top

Preheat oven to 350 degrees. In a large bowl, use a fork or other utensil to mash the bananas until they closely resemble a puree. Once the bananas are mashed well, add oil and sugar. Blend well. In a separate bowl, combine the flour, salt, baking soda, cinnamon, ginger, and cloves. Once combined well, add the flour mixture to the banana mixture. Spoon batter into your baking cups. Make them Wild Librarian-style by sprinkling raw sugar on top before placing them in the oven. You are ready to go! Bake for approximately 20–25 minutes, depending on the size of the muffins. To make sure the muffins are ready, insert a toothpick near the center of one. If the toothpick comes out clean, you know they are done! If any batter sticks to the toothpick, they need to bake for longer.

PERFECT PAIRING: Take yourself to the grass, remove your shoes, recline for a bit, and then sit and feel your bare feet against the grass and earth as you dive into a spicy banana muffin while reading Walt Whitman's poetry. Stella recommends the final section of "I Sing the Body Electric" for your full-body experience! (Warning: Don't try this on your lunch break, since you may feel too high to return to work.)

Love Walks into the Bakery

"Lucky Seven! Our Seventh Year!" was seen everywhere at the Wild Librarian the year of the seventh anniversary. It was printed on the bakery boxes, on a large banner that hung from the rafters, and even on the to-go coffee cups.

By the seventh year, the business was a smooth-sailing ship, allowing Stella to make changes at work and home. Grace and Andy, her loyal employees from the beginning, were still with her. Stella had hired additional staff, including a few former students from the college where she previously worked, to help with baking, ordering, and service. She also sold the old townhome where she had lived for most of her librarian career and bought a cottage-style 1930s home on Louise Street in the Washington Square neighborhood, not too far from Mary Chin's old home by the schoolyard. For good luck, she painted her home like the bakery with a sky-blue exterior and purple door.

Stella's new home, coupled with time away from the long hours she used to spend at the bakery, allowed her to cultivate a lush garden that was significantly more abundant than the small plot of land she had at her townhome. This also gave Jane and Henry a much larger area to play and explore. Stella planted lavender, rosemary, oregano, lemongrass, and sage and used much of her space for food plants and trees: blueberries, grapes, apples, oranges, avocados, lemons, tomatoes, and olives. It was a baker's paradise since she often harvested organic fruits and spices from her home to use for baking experiments. The walkway from the sidewalk to her front door was lined with California poppies. On a whim, she went to the hardware store one afternoon and selected the richest shade of magenta she could find to paint the step leading to her front door.

In the evenings, after working at the bakery or cultivating her garden, she took luscious baths in her vintage-style tub while Jane and Henry waited in the hallway. Then the three of them would get ready for bed. They snoozed while Stella read or watched movies.

She wasn't too far from turning sixty. Her body was sometimes a little stiff in the mornings, and it took her a moment to stretch out the kinks if she had been overly active in the garden the day before. Her unruly golden hair had grown gray highlights, and these random hairs were even more untamed. "It's your wise crone-in-training halo!" Elly Kim, her friend from the Women Who Run With the Wolves Book Club, proclaimed. Stella felt pride mingled with joy. When she thought of her life and the community she served, she was grateful. She didn't believe anything was missing.

It was just an ordinary Wednesday on an ordinary week of the seventh year when Stella told everyone she would be away for a few minutes to pick up an order from Riviera's Spice Shop next door. She returned to the Wild Librarian carrying a box of jars. Andy was talking with a customer near the bookshelves.

"Ah, here she is! Stella, I was just explaining to this gentleman about the book selection and how it's curated." Andy took the box from Stella and nodded toward the man. "Please remind me of your name."

"Chris Sosa." He extended his hand to Stella.

"Stella Peabody. It's nice to meet you. Is this your first time here?"

"It is. I was just telling him I stopped in to grab coffee. I have a work assignment nearby at the old building near 2nd and Broadway."

"I know it well," Stella said. "There are some lovely galleries in that building."

Andy left them alone to take the spices to the stockroom. Stella looked at the man. She noticed his hair was just like hers, tangled and unruly, but black with gray near his temples. He had it loosely tied back. It was quite thick and marvelous hair on an older man.

"So, Andy, if I have his name right . . ."

"Yes, Andy."

"He was telling me that you used to be a librarian. My mom is a retired librarian."

"How wonderful," Stella said, trying not to stare at his hair. "What kind of librarian?"

"A public librarian. She worked for Los Angeles County. My brother and I practically grew up in the library."

"I did too," Stella said. "My mom always took me and my brother. So, it sounds like your mom is still alive?"

"Yes, it's quite a blessing. My dad has passed, but my mom is eighty-five and going strong. Still reads up a storm. She lives with my brother and his wife."

Stella felt a tug on her heart. It was such a long time ago that she lost her mom.

The man made a motion toward the bookshelves. "No doubt she would love all this."

"Oh, yes, I'm sure," Stella said.

There was a moment of silence. Stella, usually talkative and at ease with keeping up conversations, felt unusually nervous. The man—did he say his name was Chris?—shifted his legs. *It's not just his hair*, Stella thought. *Everything about this man is attractive.* She moved her toes inside her boots while feeling an awkward lump in her throat. The silence continued until one of the staff members turned on the radio. Stella exhaled, realizing she had been holding her breath, as the music filled the bakery. It was a Nina Simone song. Stella couldn't recall the title.

"'How Long Must I Wonder,'" the man said.

"Excuse me?"

"This song. Such a great one. 'How Long Must I Wonder.' Nina Simone. Do you know it?"

"I do." Stella couldn't think of anything else to say. She looked into the man's face. He was looking intently at her. Stella became more nervous as their eyes met and locked. She noticed his eyes were almost as dark as his hair. She could feel the air thick around them, and she sensed each second ticking.

He smiled. "Well, I'll be on my way. I'm glad I stopped in." He took a sip of his coffee. "You certainly have an awesome place."

Stella watched him walk across the bakery, open the door, and begin down the sidewalk. Nina Simone was singing away. Andy looked on with curiosity as Stella scurried her way to the door and stepped onto the sidewalk, focusing on the direction of the man.

She stood watching him walk to the next block. Like his marvelous hair, she noted he had a marvelous walk. *What would you call that?* she wondered. *A swagger. Yes, a gentle swagger.* She giggled when thinking of the word and was startled when he suddenly turned around, looking in her direction. She knew he couldn't hear her, but could he see her? Stella was embarrassed. What should she do? He had stopped and seemed to be looking directly at her, but he was too far away for her to be certain. Then he raised his right arm and waved. She realized he must have spotted her. Raising her arm too, she waved back before moving quickly into the bakery.

"What was that about?" Andy asked. "Is everything okay?"

Stella stood with a large smile but didn't say anything. Andy saw how wide her eyes were. Her face was flushed.

"What's gotten into you? You look goofy!" He laughed.

Stella reached up and touched her hair. It felt puffy. "Do you remember his name?" she asked.

"Yes, Chris Sosa."

"Right! Right!" Stella said, making her way toward her office. She heard Andy in the distance.

"Did you hear his voice? Wow, that guy could do voice-overs . . ."

Stella closed the door to her office. "Chris Sosa. Chris Sosa," she said out loud. She could barely get a hold of herself. It wasn't just that he was an attractive man; there was something else. She giggled and swirled around in her chair, wondering if he'd sensed something too or if it was all in her head. Had he just found her strange? She wasn't sure what to make of the whole encounter, but she believed he would return. She would see him again.

Chris didn't return the following day, nor the day after that, but in the late morning of the next day, Saturday, he came in accompanied by an elderly woman. Stella rarely worked Saturdays any longer, but a large book shipment had arrived the day before. She was busy arranging the bookshelves and delighting in surprise as she opened each box to reveal the books inside. She turned to look toward the entrance when she heard the noise of the street. There was Chris. He approached Stella along with the woman she assumed was his mom.

"See, this is the place, and here's the woman I mentioned. The librarian," Stella heard him explaining. "Stella, I was hoping you would be here today. I wanted to bring my mom—as you know, a librarian like you—to see the bakery and the books."

Chris's mom used a cane and walked slowly, but she had a hearty glow, and her eyes were sharp and clear. Stella noticed her smart navy pantsuit and her heart soared. She thought of how wonderful it must be for Chris to still have his mom. She studied his face again, noting some lines here and there. She took him for around her age.

"Hello," the woman said to Stella. "I'm Helen."

"Helen, it's wonderful to meet you." Stella took Helen's hand inside both of hers. The old woman's eyes were dark like Chris's. She was wearing a red scarf around her short gray hair.

The three of them sat together while Grace brought coffee.

"Mmm," Helen said after sipping her coffee. "You make a good cup."

"I think you need a treat with that, right?" Stella smiled.

Helen looked at Chris.

"We'll get him something too." Stella laughed. "On the house for new customers."

Helen took a few more sips of her coffee. "Do you have anything with blueberries?"

"Oh, yes! That's one of our staples."

Grace overheard and brought a wild blueberry muffin for Helen.

"And what about you?" Stella looked at Chris. He was staring at his phone.

"My apologies. I'm waiting for an important message and wanted to make sure I didn't miss it." He dropped his phone in the large front pocket of his flannel shirt and looked at his mom who was gobbling up her muffin. Stella delighted in seeing her eat with such gusto.

"These are actually called Wild Women Blueberry Muffins, inspired by the book *Women Who Run With the Wolves*. Do you know it?" Stella asked Helen.

"Oh my. I don't think I'm familiar."

"We always have copies here. We'll get you one before you leave." Stella smiled at Chris.

"So, what about you? Blueberries too?"

"How about chocolate? I'm always up for anything with chocolate—if you have it."

Stella stepped away and brought back an On the Road Chocolate Cupcake. "Chocolate and more chocolate," she told him, referring to the cake and frosting. "This one is inspired by Jack Kerouac's novel *On the Road*. One of my favorites growing up."

Chris ate like his mom. The muffin was gone in three bites. "I know it," he said. "I had a Beat Generation phase in high school. Kerouac. Ginsberg."

"Me too!" Stella laughed.

"I can't believe that was vegan," he said, pointing to his empty plate. "The man the other day, Andy, he explained everything is vegan. Incredible. How is it so moist?"

"There's a secret ingredient in that cupcake. Something very common, actually, but you'll have to get to know me better to find out what it is."

Chris laughed. "I've never been much of a baker," he told Stella. "But I can cook."

"Chris is a great cook!" Helen confirmed.

In his mom's presence, Stella was able to act more like her regular self. She was thankful.

Chris left Stella and Helen to talk while he perused the bookshelves. Stella stayed focused on Helen, but she could sense Chris close by as if his energy filled the space. Her neck felt warm, and she had a tingling sensation throughout her body. After several minutes, he returned to the table. He had a copy of *Women Who Run With the Wolves* for his mom. He held the book with both hands. Stella wasn't sure she had ever seen such beautiful hands. They were perfectly shaped and sized. She could hear her heart pounding in her ears. Rita's story about her heartbeat on her pilgrimage to Big Sur popped into her mind. She thought of the redwood trees and imagined the ocean in the distance. Her mind was drifting.

The front door opened, and the elderly couple the McDaniels entered. Eleanor McDaniels' walking stick vibrated along the floor. "Good morning, Stella!" Eleanor called out. And just like that, Stella was pulled back into reality.

"Good morning, you two!" Stella yelled over to them and then looked at Chris.

"I'll take it," he said, tapping the book with his finger. "And we'll be on our way—right, Mom?"

Helen began organizing herself to get up. Chris came around the table to assist her. "We're going grocery shopping next," he told Stella.

"How about another muffin for later?" Helen asked.

"Of course," Stella said, leaving them to go to the bakery case. She reached behind to get a box, and when she turned around, Chris was there at the register being rung up by Grace for the book. Stella reached across the counter to hand him the box. She could feel her heart pounding again. The heat was riding up her neck.

She watched Chris and Helen leave. Once the front door closed, she said, "Oh my," and then, "Oh my. Wow!" She placed her hands on the counter to steady herself and let out an exuberant laugh. "Oh boy!"

Grace watched Stella. "Stella, look at you! Who is that man?"

"Chris Sosa."

"Someone you know?"

"Not yet."

"Not yet? What does that mean?" Grace studied Stella's face. She saw what Andy had described as "goofy."

Stella closed her eyes, inhaling and exhaling deeply.

"My goodness," was all Grace said. She rang the bell next to the cash register, making Stella laugh again, and proceeded to fan Stella's red face with a small "Lucky Seven! Our Seventh Year!" sign from the top of the bakery case.

Stella drove up to Hollywood the day after her second encounter with Chris. She was meeting Barbara and Sheila from the Women Who Run With the Wolves Book Club for a movie at an independent theater on Sunset. She arrived early and wandered into a clothing shop downstairs.

There were a lot of flowing clothes, capes, and tunics for sale in the shop. Stella thought of Clare Fortune who taught art workshops at the Wild Librarian. This store was Clare's style—but then Stella found something. Near the back of the store, she came across a black V-neck polished cotton tunic. It was simple and elegant. She ran her hand over the soft fabric. It felt luxurious in comparison to the work shirts and T-shirts she generally wore.

Having a few more minutes to spare, Stella went into the tiny dressing room and tried it on. It was perfect with her jeans. She looked at herself in the dressing room mirror, running her hands down her shoulders and over her hips, feeling her body fill out the soft fabric. The store's bright lights illuminated her hair in the small space. She saw the contrast of the black fabric with her golden hair and heard Elly's voice in her mind: "It's your wise crone-in-training halo!" Stella smiled. She felt full of anticipation. Something inside of her was awakening.

She met Sheila and Barbara outside the theater.

"What's in the bag?" Sheila asked.

"A tunic."

"A tunic?" Barbara asked. "What for?"

"For me," Stella said.

There was no way she could explain to them the true reason she'd bought the tunic. Stella was always telling everyone she was "blissfully single," so how could she explain she'd bought the item to wear on her first date with Chris, a man she'd had two brief encounters with and who had not even asked her out? It would sound like magical thinking. Even Stella was puzzled by it all. After not having an interest in a man for many years, she was suddenly full of exhilaration and a stirring of sexual energy. As she sat there in the dark theatre with Barbara and Sheila, Stella held the bag containing the tunic close to her like a prized possession. She knew she would be going out with Chris and that it would be soon. During her drive back to Santa Ana, she kept the bag on the passenger seat so she could dip her fingers inside to grab and handle the soft fabric.

Chris called the Wild Librarian the following Wednesday after the tunic purchase. He had no idea the garment was hanging on display in Stella's bedroom, waiting patiently, like she was, for the moment to arrive. And then it happened. "Would you like to have dinner with me sometime soon?" A date was set. They were going to meet at the bakery Saturday evening and go next door for dinner at Luna's Italian Restaurant.

The morning of her date, Stella dug in the back of her closet to find a pair of black boots she had worn only a handful of times. The last time was for her friend Rita's wedding at the bakery. The boots had a thick layer of dust on them. Jane, always curious, walked up, sniffed them, and sneezed. Stella took the boots to her back porch, where she brushed them off with a rag. "Just like new," she told the dogs.

She spent the rest of her morning sitting in the garden with Jane and Henry. Tall, stunning sunflowers she'd planted from seeds had bloomed and were lining the wood fence that ran along one side of her back yard. She sipped her coffee, watching the sunflowers and then turning her head to take in the vibrant red bougainvillea blossoms along the other side. The sun was already warm, bringing up the aromas of sage, rosemary, and lavender. Stella breathed it all in. She thought of the evening ahead and laughed to the dogs who were in the beginning of their post-breakfast naps, "What am I doing?" She pushed aside some hesitation and tilted her head back, feeling the sunlight on her neck and face.

Stella arrived at the bakery a few minutes before seven that night. Rodrigo, the evening manager she'd hired last year, was talking with a large group of adults and children when she walked in. She was surprised to find Robert Gonzales, normally an early-morning guest, sitting in his usual spot near the window.

"Robert!" Stella approached him. "What brings you here on a Saturday evening?"

"I just felt like getting out a bit." He looked at Stella. Something was different about her. It wasn't just her sun-kissed face; she was wearing eye shadow and a different style of clothing. He looked at the black tunic that ended at her thighs. Instead of her regular construction boots, he saw she was wearing polished black boots under her jeans. "Stella," he said, "you look lovely."

"Thank you, Robert. I have a date!"

"A date?" Robert knew Stella enough to know this was a rarity.

"I know," she said, laughing. "Can you believe it? I can't even recall the last time. He'll be here any minute."

"Stella, I'm surprised!"

"Me too!"

Robert kept looking at Stella, which made her smile. Did she see something like excitement appear in his eyes?

"What's his name?"

"Chris! Chris Sosa."

Robert saw how saying his name made Stella's face light up. "You look good, Stella," he said, moving his hands forward on the table. He continued, "Stella, you're a great woman."

"Robert!" Stella was surprised. The tone of his voice and the look on his face carried traces of his former happier self before his wife Maria left him.

"You've changed since leaving the college and opening this place," he continued. "You've become even more beautiful. More fully who you are."

Stella was stunned to receive these compliments and feel the old warmth of friendship between them that had waned in the shadow of his depression.

"You give us all hope. Even me. I can't say hope for what yet, but it's there. Far deep inside." He placed his hand flat against his chest.

This was one of the best things she'd heard Robert say in years. She was deeply moved and reached down to grasp his hands within both of hers, surprised to find how strong his hands felt. "That was beautiful to hear," Stella told him. "Thank you. Thank you so much, Robert." Her mind traveled several years back to when Robert was filled with joy and they had shared many lunch hours together on campus. "I heard from Andy and Grace that you returned to your swimming classes," she said.

"I did!" Robert took his hands from Stella's and made motions with his arms.

Stella laughed and saw Robert's face come even more alive. She was so caught up in the moment that she didn't see Chris come in.

"Stella?" She heard his voice behind her.

Stella turned to see Chris in a dark blue sweater and tan pants. She took in his hair, his eyes, and the way his hands rested in front of him. The heat sensation started, and she knew her face was getting flushed.

"Chris," she began, turning partway toward Robert, "this is my old friend and faithful customer, Robert Gonzales. We worked together at the community college where I was a librarian before opening the bakery."

Chris reached over to grab Robert's hand. They made their introductions, and Robert could not hide his enjoyment as he took everything in and watched Stella interact with Chris.

"Well, we should probably head over," Chris said. "Are you ready?"

"I am." Stella reached down and grabbed one of Robert's hands again before retrieving her bag, which she'd placed on the chair next to him.

Luna's was crowded as it often was on Saturday evenings. Stella, who was known by all the employees at the restaurant, was given one of the best tables in the house. Elise Luna, the owner, came over.

"Working on a Saturday?" Stella asked her.

"Oh, not really," Elise said. "I should have told you when you made the reservation! We have a great Cuban band performing tonight. They begin in about an hour. That's why I'm here." She moved her body in a little dance then looked at Chris, and Stella made introductions. Before walking away, she caught Stella's eye and winked.

They reviewed the large menu, but Stella already knew what she would be getting: pasta with marinara sauce and a side of sourdough bread with no butter.

"Really?" Chris asked. "Out of this large menu, that's all you want?"

"Oh yes. It's delicious. And remember,"—she pointed to herself—"vegan."

"I see. So, not just the bakery, but all the time?"

"One hundred percent. For over twenty years now."

"Okay then. Vegan it is." Chris kindly ordered the same. They shared a bottle of red wine.

In a short amount of time, Stella discovered a great deal. Chris had been divorced many years from his only marriage, which was short-lived. He had no children but was an uncle to his brother's three daughters. He was in his late fifties like Stella. His mother, Helen's, family was originally from Sicily, and his father's family was Argentinian. Chris had been born right in the heart of Los Angeles. He was a graphic designer, with most of his assignments taking him to LA every day, but he lived only a few miles from Stella in Tustin in an old building that had been converted into lofts. He gestured with his hands as he talked, becoming more expressive with the wine. He would sometimes reach up to rearrange the tie in his hair, letting it fall open for a second. Stella felt the heat begin near the base of her spine and travel up to her neck as she watched him. She was thankful for the wine, which helped to calm her nerves.

Near the middle of their meal, the Cuban band arrived and began setting up. The indoor stage area was illuminated with several sets of tiny string lights. By the time they'd finished eating, the band was in full swing. Some people got up to dance. Stella saw Elise Luna dancing with her husband. Chris stood and offered his hand to Stella. As they walked to the dance floor, he placed his arm around her, his hand gently on her elbow.

Stella hadn't danced this close to a man in many years. She felt Chris's arms around her and his hands touching the soft fabric of the tunic on her back. The music was loud. Stella could feel her heart pounding as she got closer to Chris, his body against hers for the first time. Her head fit perfectly within the bend of his arm. The movement, the wine, the rhythm of the music, and the party atmosphere carried her away. She reached both her arms up and touched Chris's hair. It was almost as she imagined, but softer. She let her fingers move within the thick waves and curls and felt dizzy. *What is happening to me?* she wondered as she completely let go and felt her full self fall into the moment.

Before leaving Luna's, Stella took a few minutes to try to gather herself in the restroom. Her head was swirling, and her emotions were going in various directions. Chris commented on the light from the bright moon when they stepped outside.

They decided to go for a short walk. A few blocks in, they were in front of the twenty-four-hour laundromat. The bright fluorescent lights from inside lit up the sidewalk.

"Well, look at that," Chris said, pointing to the laundromat.

Stella turned her head. There were a few people inside going about the expected routines, but there was a couple dancing near the wide center aisle. Stella couldn't believe what she was seeing. It was the elderly couple the McDaniels. Frank was holding Eleanor tightly in his arms as they made their way twirling up and down the aisle. At one point, Eleanor arched her back while Frank held his arms locked around her waist. Stella watched as her large breasts moved with her like two hanging domes. She was wearing an old apron that zipped up the back. Stella saw Eleanor's walking stick resting up against one of the washing machines.

They stood outside watching the McDaniels, who were undoubtedly lost in their own romantic world under the laundromat's industrial lighting. Here and there clothes spun around in dryers. People pushed carts down the aisle around them. It was quite a spectacle.

"I've seen them before," Chris said.

"Yes, of course, at the bakery. It's the McDaniels. They've been coming in since I opened." Stella was overcome with love for them, perhaps not realizing until that moment how devoted they were to each other and the passion they must share. It was hard to pull away, but they continued on with their walk while Eleanor and Frank danced.

"I'm so glad I saw that," Stella said. Chris took her hand. Sensations moved through Stella that she hadn't felt for a long time, but those earlier sensations from years ago paled in comparison to the electr city charging through her now.

As they made their way down the sidewalk, Stella began to hear something in the distance. She stopped walking.

"Is scmething wrong?" Chris asked.

"No," Stella said, turning her head at an angle. "Listen."

They stood silently for a moment.

"Do you hear it?" Stella asked.

Chris also turned his head. "I do. It's lovely," he told her. "Where do you think it's coming from?"

Stella looked far off in the opposite direction from where they were walking. In the distance, she could see a silhouette of a figure sitting on a city bench. A few people were gathered around.

"Right there,"—she pointed—"under the streetlamp. It's Guy Mandal playing his accordion."

Now that they were intently listening, they were able to hear more nuances of the music.

"I can almost make it out," Chris said. "Yes . . . of course. It's 'La Vie En Rose.' This is one of my mom's favorite songs."

"Guy calls himself a traveling musician," Stella said, smiling, "but he must have arrived here almost seven years ago now. He showed up at the bakery not too long after I opened to offer his services."

"Accordion playing? I imagine his skills must have been mismatched for a bakery bookstore," Chris said.

"Not at all," Stella told him. "I've hired him many times to play music over the years. He actually came to the right place."

Chris looked at Stella, finding her curious and beguiling. "Maybe you are the main reason he's stayed so long," he said.

"Oh, I don't know about that." Stella laughed. "There are so many good things about Santa Ana." She made a gesture with her hand, reaching out from her side. Chris moved closer and took her hand as they continued their walk.

Standing by her car later with Chris in front of her, some of

Stella's nervousness returned. Was he going to kiss her? Had she made a mistake earlier by touching his hair? She was afraid she couldn't remember how to kiss a man. She didn't know if she was ready. The confidence Chris exuded made her feel both safe and a bit self-conscious. A car passed them, playing loud mariachi music. Someone let out a cheer from inside.

Chris studied Stella. Her golden hair fell in wisps around her shoulders. He reached out and touched her arm. He could sense something like fear or caution about her, but also desire.

"This feels beautiful," he said, feeling the fabric. "And you're so beautiful," he told her. He leaned in and kissed the side of her face.

They both felt the electricity between them. The sensation overwhelmed Stella. She was thankful when Chris moved back. They said good night and parted.

Only a few days passed before they were together again. And then again. These encounters were often short walks when Chris came by the Wild Librarian. He was still local several days a week while finishing up the assignment off Broadway. Stella asked him over the phone to go slow. "It's overwhelming for me," she explained, "but I'm so happy." Another time, Chris came briefly to see her home, meet Jane and Henry, and tour her garden. They walked over to the large grouping of sunflowers. Lining the bark pathway near their feet were thick clusters of Santa Barbara daisies.

"This is crazy," Chris said. "It's a small sunflower forest. These are taller than me." He looked up at the sunflowers that bobbed their large heads in the light breeze.

Stella spread her arms out. "I call all of this my poet's garden."

"Do you write poetry?"

"No, not at all." Stella laughed. "But I love to read it."

Chris looked at Stella. Long pendant earrings caught the sunlight within her golden hair. He noticed a few gray wisps along her hairline. "You can be a poet without writing poetry," he told her.

"You think so?"

"Definitely. It's a way of life. How you see the world."

"Huh." Stella smiled. "I like that a lot."

Chris next called Stella early on a Saturday, asking her to come to his home for breakfast. When he opened the door, she handed him a bakery box. He held the box up to his nose.

"I don't even need to open it," he said. "I can smell the chocolate."

"I made a quick stop at the bakery. Did I tell you one of my personal mottos is, 'Chocolate before noon?'"

Chris laughed. "I couldn't agree more. These will be our dessert after breakfast."

Chris's loft was mostly one large space with a kitchen and living room. He had several handsomely carved bookshelves along a wall with a fireplace. A few books were piled up on the floor near a chair. She took this as an "in progress" or "read soon" pile. She had several such piles at her own home.

Chris showed her around the loft. Stairs led to the bedroom space that hovered above the kitchen. The ceiling had exposed wood rafters. Stella commented on how it felt like a cabin. There was a small patio out back. They sat together on a wooden bench off from his kitchen to eat.

Chris prepared breakfast burritos using potatoes, avocados, bell peppers, tomatoes, onions, and blackened tofu instead of eggs. He set two extra bowls in front of them—one of fresh salsa, and one full of extra avocado slices. Stella watched Chris add several more helpings of avocado to his plate. She ran her hand over the table and the back of the bench where they sat.

"It's gorgeous," she said, admiring the wood. "A work of art, actually."

"This is an old table I refinished from my parents' home."

They were silent for a moment as they both felt an energy and anticipation between them. The neighborhood and the street outside were quiet as if everyone was still sleeping. Stella could hear the ticking of Chris's wristwatch.

"Would you like me to put on music?" he asked.

"Oh, no," she said. "I like this. Maybe later?"

After they ate, Chris got up for a moment to pour more coffee into Stella's cup. Then they remained sitting at the table. Stella pushed her body back, relaxing against the bench. Chris started to talk about a current work assignment with a new clothing store opening in Venice Beach. He was designing the logo and having some difficulties with the store owner. When he spoke, Stella could feel a vibration along her back. She was mesmerized, feeling each word move through her. She closed her eyes and breathed deeply, trying to stay focused on what he was saying.

"Is everything okay?" he asked. "Are you sleepy?"

"No, no," Stella said, opening her eyes. "I feel good, relaxed. Your voice is so deep I can feel it vibrating in the wood."

Chris saw Stella's chest rise as she inhaled. He moved close and kissed her.

It was a long and intense kiss, and Stella felt a warm sensation shoot through her body. Her stomach jumped. She became lightheaded. Chris moved back.

"Just give me a moment," Stella said, looking across the room to where she could see out his window. The marine layer had lifted, and everything was covered in the late morning sunlight. She remembered how her dad used to call this type of weather a "California morning." A couple came by walking a large dog. They were walking slowly, allowing the dog to sniff everything. A delivery truck passed by.

Stella looked at Chris. Then she started to giggle. The giggle turned into an expansive laugh that filled her entire body. Chris started laughing along with her. He wasn't sure why, but it felt good and refreshing.

"Okay," Stella said once the laughter had settled and she'd caught her breath, "I'm ready for more."

Chris stood up and grabbed Stella's hand. She knew what was going to happen. She was nervous, but she no longer wanted to fight the sensations rippling through her body. She followed him up the stairs to his bedroom, where they stayed the whole day except for short ventures into the kitchen.

It was late when Stella woke from a nap in Chris's bed. She saw the night sky from a window up high in the loft.

"Oh my God! I've forgotten about Jane and Henry. I need to get home and let them out. They need dinner!" She jumped up.

"Would you like me to come with you?" he asked.

And then they were at Stella's feeding the dogs and throwing balls for them in the back yard, until they went into Stella's bedroom where they stayed the rest of the night. In the morning, they stood in Stella's kitchen drinking coffee, eating thick sourdough bread with blackberry jam, and then nibbling at a chocolate bar. When they finished, Chris held his arms out, slightly bent, in front of him.

"You can't be serious!" Stella laughed. She could tell Chris wanted to try to carry her.

"Get on," he said, keeping his arms ready.

Stella put her arms around Chris's shoulders, and he picked her up. They laughed the whole way to the bedroom as he stumbled down the hallway bumping into the walls. They stayed in bed most of the day, and then all evening, and into the morning until Chris left to get ready for work.

Before leaving, he brought Stella coffee and sat on the side of her bed. He looked down at her. Stella's hair was tangled and spread across her pillow. He touched the side of her face.

"Wow," he said.

"I know!"

When he left, she pulled the comforter up around her and ran her hands over her body, feeling all the places Chris had touched. She rolled over and found her cell phone on the nightstand. She called the bakery. Grace answered.

"Grace, it's Stella. I won't be coming in today. Can you all get along without me?"

"Are you ill?" Grace asked. Her concern warmed Stella's heart. She couldn't remember the last time she hadn't made it in to the bakery.

"No, not ill," Stella said, and then she started to giggle and move her feet around in the bed. "Far from ill." She laughed. "If you know what I mean! I just need to rest some."

"My, my . . ." Grace laughed back, thinking of Chris. "Good for you, Stella! Good for you!"

Stella pulled the pillow Chris had lain on close to her. She could smell his hair. Her heart started to race, and she felt a roller coaster sensation from her belly to her chest. And then she lay there for a while and cried. It was a good cry, not a cry of sadness. A cry that came from bliss and unexpected happiness.

That evening, she could no longer keep her story to herself. She placed a call to Seattle. Her brother, Ben, answered.

"Ben," Stella told him, "I've met a man."

Stella spent her day of relaxation after her weekend of ecstasy experimenting in her kitchen. In her bathrobe during the afternoon, she foraged through her well-stocked pantry considering various spices from her garden and others from Riviera's. Inspiration hit when she saw a half-full bottle of dark rum sitting next to a container of shredded coconut. By evening, she had perfected a coconut rum cake drizzled with a butter rum glaze, which she made by boiling sugar, vegan butter, rum, and vanilla in a small saucepan on the stove.

Stella got into bed after a long bubble bath in her favorite rose milk. She rubbed her hands along the side of the bed where Chris had been and then put her face close to the sheet and inhaled his lingering scent. She adjusted the pillows behind her and grabbed the dish with rum cake on the nightstand. Henry was curled up at the foot of the bed, looking at her with his brown eyes, hoping for a taste. Jane appeared sniffing alongside the bed.

"Come on, old girl." Stella tapped the bed.

Jane jumped up and lay down near Henry.

Along with her soft lamp on the nightstand and the moonlight coming through the window, Stella ate her second slice of the cake. What could she call her creation? It wasn't inspired by a book. There wasn't an author she could associate it with. No, this was clearly a cake insp red by Chris. Then she knew. Of course. Lover's Cake.

☕

"Would you like to go with me?" Stella asked Chris, showing him information about a museum exhibit on her phone. They had been together several months and were spending a night or two during the week and most of their weekends together.

Chris was a hit with the staff and regulars at the Wild Librarian. Stella had enjoyed a few meals with his mother Helen, his brother David, and David's wife Laura. All of them met and loved Jane and Henry. Stella could feel her life expanding in a way she hadn't imagined, but she tried to take things one day at a time and not get too carried away with dreams and fantasies unfolding in her imagination. It was enough, she told her herself, to enjoy each experience with Chris anc his family for the joy it brought in the moment.

Chris scanned the information on Stella's phone. They were sitting inside the bakery early in the morning before he started his drive to see a client in Manhattan Beach. "It's at LACMA? Definitely. How about next Friday? You don't work Fridays anymore, and I'll take the day cff."

On Friday, they left Santa Ana shortly after 9:00 a.m. to miss most of the rush-hour traffic. It was only a little past ten when they found parking and started walking toward the Los Angeles County Museum of Art. The museum's feature exhibit Stella wanted to see was a showcase of art by surrealist women artists in Mexico and the United States.

They walked through the exhibit rooms together. There was art by Fr da Kahlo, Leonora Carrington, Remedios Varo, and many others. Stella's favorite part was a large panel that featured photos and biographical information about each woman.

Chris looked at Stella's face as she read about the artists. "How are you feeling?" he asked.

"Dazzled," she said, which made Chris laugh and embrace her.

The museum's new outdoor bar was open, so they found a table and ordered wine. The day was overcast. Chris looked at Stella's eyes. They seemed to change color depending on the light. Were they blue? Gray? He moved his chair around the table to be next to her, draping his arm up around the top of her chair. There had been a lot of people at the exhibit, but it was quiet at the bar, except for some passing conversations of other visitors. Stella leaned back. Chris's hand was near her ear, and it was quiet enough that she could hear the soft ticking of his wristwatch.

Before making the drive back, they walked down near the corner of the boulevard to look inside the craft and folk art museum.

"Oh, look!" Stella called out. "Paper mache!"

"Those are great," Chris said.

There were bowls and various objects for sale in the gift shop. Stella picked them up, feeling how light they were in her hands. Some were painted entirely in vibrant colors, and others still revealed the newspaper that had been used to construct them. Chris walked around the first floor and returned to the gift shop, surprised to see Stella still examining the paper mache.

"You really like them," he commented.

"I do. I've always wanted to try."

"Why don't you then?"

Stella didn't answer for a while, considering. She picked up one of the bowls. It was turquoise and had a pink heart painted inside. She looked at Chris. "I guess I never found the time and it would slip my mind. Other things were more pressing," she told him.

"Did you do it in elementary school?'

"Yes, I have some memories. I've always been captivated whenever I come across something like these." She placed the bowl down.

"You get the Sunday paper, right?" he asked.

"Yes."

"Then you're all set. Maybe try an experiment this Sunday?"

While Chris drove them back to Santa Ana, Stella watched a few short YouTube videos that showed beginning methods for constructing paper mache dolls and bowls.

"Chris," she said, "stop at the grocery store. I need a balloon."

"A balloon?"

"It's a way I can make a paper mache bowl!"

Stella put aside the books and arts sections from the Sunday newspaper for later reading. This gave her the bulk of the newspaper to work with. She cleared a space on her kitchen counter and put on an apron she often wore for baking. In a large mixing bowl she combined flour, water, and a dash of salt. This would be her glue. She took scissors and cut strips from the newspaper. To keep the balloon in place, she used masking tape to affix it to another mixing bowl. She put on Joni Mitchell's *Blue*, her favorite album, and got to work.

Stella dipped the paper strips in the glue mixture as she worked to cover half the balloon in two thin layers. There was a dry desert heat, and the sun was beating down on a stretch of her garden. She set the bowl outside, washed her hands to remove the flour mixture that had stuck to her fingers, and pulled off her apron. She looked at the balloon covered in newspaper drying in her garden. It was almost like waiting for something in the oven. "Magical, huh?" she asked Henry and Jane, but they were in the midst of their afternoon naps and couldn't be bothered.

She called Chris on the phone. "The bowl is drying outside now!"

"You finished it already?"

"Yes!"

"Amazing. I don't think I can get away to come over later—I have that difficult client in Venice Beach waiting for me to finish some work. How about tomorrow morning?"

"Perfect!"

Stella drove to an art supply store Chris recommended. Stepping inside gave her a thrill. She walked the aisles. It was full of possibilities, like a new world opening. She felt a sensation move through her body—an exhilarating feeling that was similar in some ways to how she felt when she was close to Chris.

She found the acrylic paint section. Seeing all the colors, brands, and various shapes of the containers was like being at Riviera's Spice Shop. She examined them for several minutes before selecting various shades of blue, green, and purple. Stella added a tube of Renaissance Gold to her shopping basket, and then she was down another aisle looking for synthetic brushes.

Driving back home, she passed by the grocery store near the freeway exit, but then she thought of the possibilities with the paint. In her mind, she saw the mixing bowl on her kitchen counter that she hadn't yet cleaned. She knew it was still over halfway full of the glue mixture. She made a U-turn at the next light. Within a few minutes, she was in the small floral shop area of the store where they sold balloons, and then she was in line with a heart-shaped balloon that read, "I love you," two small round birthday ones, and an unusual square-shaped balloon with gold letters reading, "Best Wishes."

Back at home, Stella touched the newspaper on the balloon that was drying in the sun. It was so hot that it had already dried. She removed the balloon from the bowl and then got a safety pin to poke it. The balloon popped and shriveled up inside the newspaper. She peeled the balloon off and found herself holding her first paper mache object. It was a bit wonky here and there, but it was lovely. She balanced it in the palm of her hand and let out a cheer.

Stella set the bowl on the kitchen table and turned on the stereo to get to work on her other creations. "Yes! Yes!" she said out loud as she began.

When Chris got to her home early the next morning, he knocked and then let himself in. The dogs came running with him into Stella's bedroom. All three of them jumped on the bed, startling Stella. Jane let out a good howl.

"I've overslept!" Stella yelled. "They're going to wonder what has gotten into me at the bakery." She rubbed her eyes with both hands. "I told Andy I'd be in early to handle some ordering."

"I'm sure it can wait," Chris said. "Were you up late?" He saw Stella's eyes light up.

"I was!" She pulled herself up in bed. "Look!" She grabbed the first bowl she made from where she'd placed it on her nightstand. Chris saw how Stella had cut and trimmed the lip in a jagged manner so it resembled leaves. It was a pale green, with the tips of the leaves lightly frosted with the Renaissance Gold. Stella had been up past midnight painting it.

"Oh, wow!" Chris said as Stella handed him the bowl. It felt almost weightless in his hand. He could feel a few spots with slight bumps where she may have unintentionally made an extra layer. This added to the charm. "This is beautiful, Stella."

They went into the kitchen to make coffee and let the dogs out the back door.

"Chris, look!" she called to him, pointing out the window above the kitchen sink. Chris looked outside. At first, he wasn't sure what he was looking at. Then he started to laugh.

"My God!" he told her. "It's like a production studio."

The temperature had remained warm all night, so before going to bed, Stella had placed all her creations outside in the garden to begin drying. Jane and Henry were sniffing and investigating them. There was the large heart-shaped one, the two small bowls, and the square one.

"Let's go check." Stella grabbed Chris's hand. It wasn't yet eight o'clock, but it was already very warm and dry out. She touched the newspaper she had glued to the balloons. "Still a little damp," she said. "They'll be ready and waiting for me when I get home tonight!"

Chris looked at Stella. She was beaming outside in her white nightgown in the midst of her lush garden, and now with these paper mache objects. She held her hands together in front of her, near her heart.

Stella was helping a group of students display their works for sale on the shelves designated for local artists. Over the years since the shelves first held Maria's pottery, they'd offered various types of creations, from jewelry to handmade greeting cards.

Grace called out to her. "Stella, Chris is on the phone."

She made her way to her office, passing by Andy who was placing slices of freshly baked Lover's Cake in the bakery case.

"Hi, what's up?" she asked Chris.

"Just checking in. How's your day going?"

"Great! How about you?"

"Good. I'm going to be home around seven. How does a late dinner sound at your place?"

"I can't wait."

Chris came with wine and a bag from the grocery store. Stella got busy clearing the kitchen table, which had become her paper mache painting space. Off to the side was a growing collection of bowls and various objects painted in vibrant colors.

"I have something to show you," she told Chris, coming up behind him where he stood in front of the stove. She held up two paper mache figures, one in each hand. They were about twelve inches tall. Chris easily recognized one as Frida Kahlo. He looked at the other one. It was a woman with long blonde hair. She was holding a guitar and had a paintbrush coming out of her hair.

"Who is this one?" Chris asked.

"Joni Mitchell."

"Oh, of course. Wow." He put a spoon down on the counter and held the Frida one. Stella watched how he turned it gently in his hand. "These are amazing. What did you use?"

"Wire mesh."

"Like chicken wire?"

"Yes. A guy at the art supply store helped me find the materials when I told him what I wanted to try. And then, you see,"—she touched the side of the Joni Mitchell one—"the same process with the flour glue and newspaper."

"You must have just made them."

"Yes, over the past few nights."

"And the hair—what is it?"

"Different papers. Mostly lokta and mulberry. I discovered a whole section of dyed papers when I picked up the wire. See, I tear it," she said, lightly touching the figure, "and the fibers in the paper look like hair."

Chris examined the hair and then the faces. The faces weren't painted on, but composed with different colored papers. "The faces," he said, "they're like collage."

"I cut the dyed papers instead of tearing to make—see here—the sharp edges."

"Stella, honestly, these are really good."

"Thank you!" She took the Frida figure back from him, touching the face with her index finger. "They almost seem real to me." She laughed. "Like they have souls."

When they sat down at the table to start eating, everyone was there: Jane and Henry underneath hoping something would fall, Stella and Chris, and then Frida and Joni at the far end with the rest of Stella's creations. Chris made burritos with fresh guacamole and salsa on the side.

"You are becoming a vegan chef!"

"I suppose I am. At least when I'm here."

After eating, they sat together on the couch. Chris looked deep in thought. Stella hadn't noticed it earlier, but she now sensed he may have had a bad day at work or there was something pressing on his mind.

"It seems my mom has changed a bit," he said.

Stella immediately grew concerned. She thought of her mom and held her glass tighter. "What is it?"

Chris could hear the worry in her voice. "Oh, I don't mean to alarm you. I've been on the phone with my brother the past two days. It seems it could be nothing. Just something odd."

"She's not feeling well?"

"No, she says she feels great. She has started to ask these bizarre questions. There's a new one each day."

"What do you mean?"

"She calls them 'magical questions.'"

"Magical questions," Stella said out loud, looking down at Chris's hands. He was doing this thing he sometimes did when he was trying to figure something out. He had set his wineglass down and was moving his hands slightly back and forth on the tops of his thighs.

"Yeah. She says it's only for fun and nothing to worry about. It's just odd. We don't know why it started."

"But nothing else seems wrong?"

"Nothing at all. In fact, she's very happy."

"Give me an example. An example of one of the questions."

Chris laughed. "Okay, so, David said the question for today is, 'How many people do you think rode their bikes across the Golden Gate Bridge yesterday?'"

"Wow," Stella said. She couldn't help but smile. "I hope it is nothing because, I have to say, that's kind of spectacular. So poetic."

"Oh, yeah. They are all like that."

"And you said it's been going on for a few days?"

"I think David said four or five days now."

"So, there have been four or five questions so far?"

"Yes."

"And she doesn't seem upset or frustrated by them?"

"Not at all. We made an appointment though with her doctor. She'll have an exam in a few days."

Stella looked across the room. The dogs had moved over from the kitchen to be close to them. Jane was asleep, and Henry was lying close by watching Chris and Stella.

"I hope so much that nothing is wrong," Stella said. In her mind, she saw Helen with her sharp pantsuits and vibrant, clear eyes. "I'd love to see her again soon," she said.

Chris came into the Wild Librarian with his mom the following Tuesday night. He knew Stella would be there getting ready for her book club.

"Helen!" Stella said, grabbing Helen's hand within hers. "What a surprise! It's so wonderful to see you."

Helen was wearing a purple hat with embroidered flowers around the band. "Stella, so nice to be here in your lovely place."

Stella had a good amount of time before the book club members were due to show up, so she sat at a table with Helen and Chris after getting a blueberry muffin for Helen and a chocolate cupcake for Chris. She also brought Helen a small slice of her new creation.

"I brought you a little of this to try too," she told her. "Do you like rum flavor?"

"Oh, yes. That looks delicious."

"This is Lover's Cake," she told Helen, winking at Chris. Stella watched Helen eat with her usual gusto. "So," she began, "I heard something about these 'magical questions . . .'"

"Yes, indeed. Would you like to hear the question for today?" Helen asked.

"I would."

"How many tents do you suppose are on Mount Everest today?"

Stella clapped her hands. "Oh my!"

Helen looked at her delighted.

She took a guess: "I'm going to say seventy-two."

Helen slapped her hand on the table and threw her head back, letting out a hearty laugh. "See!" She looked at Chris while pointing at Stella. "She gets it! Unlike you and David. It's just fun!" Then she whispered to Stella, but loud enough for Chris to hear, "The boys think something is wrong with me. That I'm losing my mind. I tell them nothing is wrong with a little fun!"

"Where do the questions come from, Helen?" Stella asked.

"My imagination." Helen tapped the side of her purple hat. She then touched her finger to her tongue and proceeded to dab it on her plate to get any remaining cake crumbs.

"Would you like more?"

"Yes," she said, "more of the rum."

"Coming right up."

Chris followed Stella to the bakery case.

"She's a treasure, Chris," she told him.

"Yes, she is." He looked back at his mom, who was looking around the bakery. He saw her wave to some people at a nearby table. "But what do you think about the questions?"

"They are quite magical." Stella snickered.

"Oh, Stella." Chris looked a bit disappointed but couldn't help smiling. "Seriously."

"I'm not concerned," Stella said. "You mentioned she had a doctor's appointment coming up?"

"No, that already passed. I'm sorry I didn't tell you. It was yesterday."

"And . . .?"

"The doctor told us to relax."

Stella couldn't help but laugh. "That sounds like wise advice." She reached into the bakery case to retrieve a heftier slice of the Lover's Cake.

Elly Kim from the book club walked in and waved to Stella, taking a seat at their designated table. By the time Stella and Chris got back to Helen, Barbara and Sheila had showed up too.

"It looks like my book club is starting to gather," Stella told Helen.

"Book club?"

"Women Who Run With the Wolves Book Club."

"Oh boy," Helen said, starting to dig into her Lover's Cake. "You don't want to miss that."

Stella asked Chris for permission first. And then she asked his mom. This led to her asking permission of others—Grace, Andy and Alex, the core members of the Women Who Run With the Wolves Book Club, the McDaniels. Everyone gave their approval for Stella to transform their likenesses into one of her artful figures.

She had been making her paper mache people at the rate of two to three a week for several months, starting with writers and artists to join Frida Kahlo and Joni Mitchell. Then she knew what her heart desired: she wanted to pay tribute to those she loved. Chris, her first attempt, took three tries to get the hair right using black torn lokta paper, tiny strips of a paper bag she painted black, and a few gray strings of thin hemp yarn. She used a deep indigo to paint one of her favorite sweaters—the one he wore on their first date at Luna's. She used a dark brown mulberry paper for his eyes.

"What do you think?" she asked him, holding the figure up for his review.

Chris took it from her, laughing and looking back and forth from the figure to Stella. "I can't believe it," he said.

"Pretty good, huh?" She laughed, clapping her hands.

The figure of Chris had the honor of being with the famous writers and artists on a shelf off from her kitchen until Stella began to create and mix in others to join the growing collection. As the numbers grew, Chris started to call them her "cast of characters."

"You're one of my characters then?" She put her arms around him.

"I suppose I am." He kissed the top of her head.

Chris was looking at the collection of close to two dozen figures one night, delighting in seeing Jane and Henry had been added.

Stella had created Jane's head at an angle, as if she were letting out one of her howls. He touched the white paper she had torn into ruffled layers to create Jane's thick coat. Stella had Henry holding a bright yellow tennis ball in his mouth with his tail straight up in the air as he often appeared when playing. Stella came next to him in her nightgown. She had just emerged from a warm bath.

"Can you stay tonight?"

"Yes," he told her. "I don't need to get to LA until late morning."

"Oh, good!"

He pointed to the figure of Eleanor McDaniels. "This is one of my favorite ones," he said. "I love how she has her walking stick."

"I love that too," Stella said.

"Do you want to keep these all here?" he asked.

"I like how they're near the kitchen." She motioned in the direction. "Is it looking too cluttered? You think I should put them somewhere else?"

"Oh, no," Chris said. "I just feel they need to be seen." He put his arm around Stella. The back of her hair was wet, and he could smell the rose milk on her skin. It was now a familiar scent that simultaneously aroused and comforted him. "I think they should be at the bakery—at least the ones of your employees and customers."

"Really?"

Chris could hear the excitement starting in Stella's voice. She had never considered it.

"But where?"

"I've thought of that," he said. "There's that section of the wall where the bookshelves end, where you have that small display table. You already have Tom Donald's beautiful vision of the Wild Librarian hanging there. You could move that display table out and create a space next to Tom's art. I feel these are so special. Imagine the charm they would add."

Chris didn't need to say anymore. Stella's heart was racing. "They feel like good luck charms to me," she said, starting to imagine them gathered in the bakery.

Knowing Alex's fine craftsmanship of the Wild Librarian's bookshelves and wood furniture that had held up so well over the years, Stella had him create a large display case for the figures in the perfect place Chris suggested. Although she shared photos of the ones she'd made for each person and brought some into the bakery to show everyone as she began to create them, only Chris had seen the whole collection.

Alex designed an exquisite art-style display cabinet that perfectly matched the bookshelves. It complimented the wood frame of Tom's vision of the bakery hanging next to it.

"It's going to be wonderful," Grace said when she saw Stella looking at the empty case one day. "I can't wait."

"Thank you, Grace," Stella said.

"When will you bring them in?"

"Soon. I just have some more to make."

It was a few nights later when Stella's mind started dreaming up an idea. She was standing at the kitchen counter beginning to construct the figure that would be Tom Donald. She imagined him holding his art portfolio full of vision boards.

"I just thought of something." She looked up quickly at Chris but kept dipping a newspaper strip in the glue. She wore a huge smile.

"Something about that smile, Stella," Chris started. "Should I be worried?"

"It's about the magical questions."

"Okay." He walked over and put his arms around her from behind. Then, gently holding onto her upper arms, he whispered into her ear, "What is the artist thinking?"

Henry came scampering by with a tennis ball in his mouth.

"The questions need to be preserved and shared," Stella said. "Are they all gathered somewhere?"

"You should know the answer to that, being a librarian." Chris laughed. "David told me she has them written down by date in a notebook."

"This is my idea." Stella spun around, forgetting her fingers were dipping in the flour glue, getting some of the mixture on Chris's shirt.

He laughed and grabbed her hands.

Stella continued. "My idea is to gather all the magical questions into a small zine. You know, like a booklet or art book. You could design it!" Her voice got more excited. "It could be the Wild Librarian Bakery and Bookstore's first publication!"

"Now you're going into the publishing business?" Chris felt the tips of Stella's fingers where the glue was hardening. He looked into her eyes. She had the bright glow he now recognized as her creativity and imagination. It was the same glow that came when she thought up a new recipe. He had seen it at the folk museum too as she stood looking at the paper mache bowls.

"Do you think your mom would like that?"

"An art book with her questions." Chris kept looking at Stella. "Hmm."

"Why don't you ask her? It could be titled 'Helen's Magical Questions.'"

Chris called Stella at home a few nights later. "Stella," he said, "I have a question for you."

She waited.

"It's nice and warm here, but very cold back east. How many snowflakes do you suppose fell in Central Park today?"

Stella's heart soared. "Oh, I love it! Is that Helen's question for today?"

"Yes." He laughed.

Stella had just prepared a cup of tea. She carried it over to the couch and sat down.

"I thought about your idea. And I talked with David," Chris said.

"And . . .?"

"We talked to our mom also. You're right about this, Stella. She is overjoyed by the idea."

"I knew it! This is going to be wonderful!"

In preparation for the art book, Helen and Stella looked through Helen's notebook together one night at the bakery. The magical questions had been coming for several months now. Stella suggested they use the first one hundred for the publication. Once this was decided, Stella easily created an electronic document, and they rolled into production.

Helen selected a terracotta shade for the front cover Chris had designed. Stella got up and danced around the bakery when he sent her an image that showed how one of the front interior pages would appear. Near the center bottom, it read, "Wild Librarian Bakery and Bookstore Publications." In no time, they were ready for a book release party.

"How are the cast of characters coming?" Chris asked her over the phone one night. He had just picked up several hundred copies of Helen's book from the printer and was opening one of the boxes.

"Just finishing up Robert Gonzales," she said, "and then I think I'll have the collection complete until new characters appear. I'm so happy Robert agreed to this." She could hear the sound of Chris pulling up the flaps of a box.

"Stella," he said, "just wait till you see these." He was holding a copy of *Helen's Magical Questions*. The binding was elegantly stitched with a gold thread.

"I'm so damn excited!" Stella pushed forward to the edge of her seat. She moved her toes around.

"Let me send you a photo."

"Ahhhh!" Stella yelled into the phone once the image came through. "Gorgeous!"

"Let me tell you what I'm thinking," Chris started. "The reason I was asking about the figures, Stella, is because I think it would be great if they were unveiled at the book release party."

"Oh, I wouldn't want to take away from your mom's celebration."

"Are you kidding? She would love it. You think about it, and I'll ask her."

☕

"Join us to celebrate our eighth anniversary," the flyers read, inviting people to the combined event of Stella's art unveiling and Helen's book release. Helen had only been honored to include Stella's paper mache figures in the planned celebration.

When she was making early preparations for the event, Stella went out one day to find Guy Mandal playing his accordion at the park. She knew he had been earning enough with his music the past few years to rent a room at a residential hotel not too far from the Wild Librarian. Stella invited him to play at the anniversary celebration. In his customary way, he shyly accepted, averting his eyes from Stella.

"Guy," Stella said, "you've shared a little with me over the years. I know you've traveled a lot. You came to California from Kentucky, right?"

"That's right. A place called Bardstown."

"And before that . . ." Stella looked off to recall, "Georgia?"

"You have quite a memory, Stella. Atlanta. I got into some trouble there."

Guy had alluded to his "trouble" a few times in the past, but Stella never pried to find out more. From some scattered comments, she'd pieced together that he worked for the railroad at one point and had also served jail time. His shy disposition didn't fit with some of the pieces, but Stella wasn't bothered by the mystery. She liked Guy, and her intuition told her he was harmless.

"You've been here for quite a while now. I'm wondering if you're going to still travel. Are you planning to stay? Make this your home?"

"I haven't decided," Guy said, looking down. He pulled the straps of the accordion off his shoulders and removed it from his lap. After placing it next to him on the bench, he leaned down and tapped a buckle on one of his worn engineer boots before meeting Stella's gaze. "This place has some of the nicest people I've ever met," he said, serious and soft, but without a smile.

Stella was surprised that he continued to look at her. He was bent forward slightly, with his hands clasped together, hanging in the open space between his legs.

"Sometimes, it makes me feel like I belong," he said.

"Oh," Stella said, "you do, Guy. I knew it the minute you walked into the bakery."

There was a flurry of activity as some of the last-minute arrangements came together for the event. Stella was going over some details with Andy one morning when Robert Gonzales came in.

"On your way to swimming class soon, Robert?" Andy called out to him.

"No," Robert said. "It's been changed to Wednesdays and Fridays." He walked over to where they were standing near the bakery case. "Are you two busy in the middle of something?"

"Never too busy for you, Robert," Stella said. She noticed his face had a healthy glow. He didn't look haggard any longer. She remembered his appearance at Tom Donald's art exhibit in a new suit and how alive he had seemed the evening of her first date with Chris. He must be experiencing a turning point.

"I'm sorry to show up like this." Robert addressed Stella. "Can I talk to you for a few minutes?"

Although they had always been friendly and occasionally chatted, it was years since they'd sat together in Stella's office. Stella considered all the turmoil and drama they'd experienced in the small space that had altered their friendship. She felt a tinge of unease that they were gathered there again after his unexpected arrival, but it quickly passed. They sat together in the chairs across from Stella's desk. Stella looked at Robert. He smiled. She felt the warm pull of their old friendship as she studied his face and waited for him to speak.

"I've enjoyed coming in all these years, Stella," Robert began. "As you've probably gathered, I found myself in a deep hole. It's taken a long time to dig myself out. Sometimes, it was just coming here that kept me feeling alive."

"Oh, Robert," Stella said. "You are as much a part of the fabric of this place as I am." As she said it, Stella knew it was true.

"Thank you for being a great friend," Robert said. "In many ways, you've been my dearest friend, even if I never expressed it."

Stella thanked Robert. She sensed he was just getting started and he had much more to say.

"I've talked to Maria," Robert said.

His words cut through the air, startling Stella. Everything quickly flashed through her mind when he spoke the name of her old friend and his ex-wife: Maria's disappearance several years ago; the community's search and rallying behind Robert; the police; the discovery Maria had deserted him for another man; Robert's decline and the eventual divorce. Stella knew Maria had asked to speak with Robert back when the drama was at a high point and the divorce was pending, but Robert had always refused.

"Wow," was all Stella could say.

They were silent for a good minute before Robert began to share more. He told her Maria had continued to make occasional requests to speak to him through her attorney. Finally, a few months ago, Robert agreed. They'd shared three long conversations since then. Speaking rapidly, Robert explained that Maria had kept most of her suffering to herself during their marriage. Following menopause and believing she had waited too long to be able to adopt a baby, her mental health deteriorated as she became fixated on how she hadn't been able to have a child. She managed to put up a good front. Unbeknownst to Robert, she had started to see a psychiatrist for several months before leaving.

"You didn't notice anything?" Stella asked.

"I should have paid better attention. I found her a few times in the living room in the middle of the night, crying and mumbling to herself. She claimed it was simply related to her body changing," Robert said. "And to be honest, I now see how I only made things worse by perpetuating our romance and happiness. I was clinging to our earlier years and how I wanted things to be."

Robert shared that Maria's affair with her former ceramics professor, Malcolm Boyd, predated her mental health collapse. At first, it was not a physical relationship, but they became close as Maria relied on Malcolm as a confidant. Not long after leaving Robert and moving in with Malcolm, she was hospitalized for a short period. She called what happened "something like a nervous breakdown," Robert said.

"And then it happened again shortly after our divorce went through," he told Stella.

"A hospitalization for mental health reasons?" Stella asked.

"Yes, but a longer stay the second time. The relationship with Boyd fell apart once she was released, and she left him."

Stella discovered Maria had gotten in touch with a distant cousin outside Mexico City. She moved there for close to a year, teaching and making ceramics. She was now living in Portland, Oregon, in a shared house she rented with two other women. One of the women had a young daughter Maria helped care for.

"And is she still making her pottery?" Stella asked.

"Oh, yes." Robert smiled. "She is quite the thing. Flourishing, really. She has a tiny studio where she also holds classes, mostly for small children." He leaned back in his chair and closed his eyes. Stella saw tears were gathering. She reached over to her desk to grab the tissue box for Robert. He took one and wiped his eyes.

Although he was crying, it wasn't from sadness. It was something closer to the relief one feels when a deep understanding is reached after a period of darkness.

"Are you going to see her?" Stella asked.

"Oh, it's a long way from that. I don't know if that will ever happen or if it would even be good for either of us." He paused before continuing. "She's very happy. She wishes to stay on her own. And, Stella,"—Robert spoke slowly, as if each word carried weight—"I forgive her completely. I've told her, 'Maria, I forgive you.'"

Stella's eyes were also filled with tears by the time Robert finished. It overwhelmed her to hear Robert speak of forgiveness after all he had been through.

His story filled the space with a heaviness that began to lift until the air felt light again, and they surprised themselves by smiling through their tears, then giggling, and finally laughing hysterically.

"What are we laughing about?" Robert gasped.

Stella placed the palms of her hands on her face and tried to compose herself to answer him. "I suppose we are laughing at life," she said. "The beautiful craziness of this thing we call life."

The evening of the eighth anniversary celebration, a table was arranged for Helen to sit and sign copies of her art book. She arrived with David and his wife, Laura, wearing a burnt orange pantsuit with a golden scarf to closely mirror the colors of her book. After saying a few words about her hope that the magical questions would stimulate others and bring wonder into their day, she sat comfortably at the table among stacks of her books like a celebrity author.

Stella walked over to where Guy was set up in a corner with his accordion. She gestured for him to begin playing. A soft, warm rendition of "That's Amore" filled the space.

Stella's brother, Ben, was unable to fly down from Seattle, but he sent a large arrangement of wildflowers in a glass vase that Chris set up next to the display case holding Stella's creations. During the second hour, the unveiling of the cast of characters took place. Stella stood by the case wearing the soft black tunic from her first date with Chris. As the cloth was pulled away to reveal the more than two dozen figures, Stella's employees, customers, and friends got close to find themselves.

The core members of the Women Who Run With the Wolves Book Club, including the late Mary Chin, were together on a shelf. Stella had created a wolf figure to stand next to Mary's likeness. Tom Donald smiled when he saw how Stella had created him holding an art portfolio. She'd placed him next to Jane and Henry on the shelf.

Andy and Alex found themselves with Alex holding a black cat to resemble Mary's beloved Dr. Freud, whom they adopted after her passing. Guy was created holding an accordion Stella had fashioned out of thick cardstock. Rita Johansen laughed and hugged Stella when she saw the double goddess design from her trip to Big Sur drawn on her likeness wearing a green dress. She was also holding a book with the name "Henry Miller" painted on it. "Your dress is green like the old van going up the coast!" Stella told her.

Within an almost continuous uproar of laughter, applause, and conversation, Stella turned her head to find Robert standing off to the side and quietly viewing the display case. She took a few steps to get next to him. She had created Robert with a welding helmet in the crook of his arm, and swimming goggles in his other hand. Stella could see a tear forming in the corner of his eye.

"I love it," he told Stella, and then again. "I love it. Thank you."

Stella took Robert's hand in hers.

Helen came over and scanned the display case until she found her likeness in a figure adorned in a navy pantsuit with a purple hat. "Ha!" she exclaimed. Stella could sense her delight.

She put her arms around Helen. The two women looked at each other. Stella saw excitement in Helen's bright eyes. "I saw you busy signing away at your table," she told her.

"Chris says we've sold over one hundred copies already! I'm taking a short break."

It was crowded, and people were milling about. Stella looked toward the entrance and saw the McDaniels enter.

Chris came over to Stella and Helen. "How are the celebrities doing?" he teased.

"We're taking a break," Helen said.

"Mom, are you tired?"

"Not at all. I see a line forming," she said, nodding toward the table where she had been signing. "Go tell them I'll be right there."

Stella and Chris laughed.

Joni Mitchell's *Blue* album started playing over the stereo system. Most of the employees knew this was Stella's favorite record. Stella scanned the room until she found Grace and Andy looking at her. Andy pointed toward one of the speakers, and then they both raised their glasses in salute to her.

Chris found Stella outside with Jane and Henry the morning after the eighth anniversary celebration. The sun was just rising. She had a gray sweater pulled around her nightgown and a cup of coffee resting against her lap.

"Stella, it's early. I didn't hear you get up."

"You were sound asleep. I know how exhausted you've been with work this week."

He bent down to kiss her. "I love you," he said.

"I love you so much."

"Coffee left inside?"

"Oh, yes, a good amount."

When he came back to the garden, Stella had pulled her legs up onto her chair. She was looking up into the sky.

"Can I join you in your poet's garden?" Chris asked.

"Always." Stella smiled.

"Last night was so wonderful, wasn't it?" Chris said.

Stella smiled. "Your mom seemed so proud."

"And the paper mache figures. Stella, everyone was captivated." Chris could see tears forming in her eyes. "Is everything okay?" he asked.

"Yes," she said slowly, looking at him. Chris's face opened into a tired smile.

Stella returned to gazing upward. Her mind began a journey. She thought of the Wild Librarian and how it must look now, so lovely and mysterious in the dark while anticipating the morning rush. The cast of characters would soon be illuminated in the display case when

Grace arrived to turn on the lights. She thought of her core book club members going strong all these years—Elly, Barbara, Sheila. She imagined Mary in the goddess spaceship eating Taos Bread. She saw Commander walking in the tall Montana grass at the wolf sanctuary and thought of Tom Donald making his vision boards in his tiny apartment. In her mind, she saw Guy Mandal on a park bench beneath a purple jacaranda tree, playing his accordion. She smiled seeing Rita and the green van making its way to Big Sur. She thought of Robert, swimming laps and becoming stronger, and his beloved Maria up in Portland teaching children in her pottery studio. And the McDaniels' late-night dance in the laundromat. She thought of her brother in Seattle and her parents gracefully balancing somewhere in space. She wondered if Helen was awake and if she already knew what the magical question was for today. And then she thought of the first time she saw Chris at the bakery. She remembered how she knew he would return. She turned to see his marvelous hair and his beautiful hands holding his coffee. He was quietly watching her.

"Yes. Yes," she said. "Everything is definitely okay."

On the Road Chocolate Cupcakes
Recipe for 12 regular-size cupcakes

1 1/2 cups unbleached organic flour
1 teaspoon organic vanilla extract
1 cup organic raw sugar
1 tablespoon organic white vinegar
3 tablespoons organic cocoa
1 cup water
1/2 teaspoon salt
6 tablespoons organic oil
1 teaspoon baking soda

Preheat oven to 350 degrees. Mix dry ingredients together first. Add wet ingredients to the dry mix until the batter is even. Don't overmix! Pour batter into baking cups and bake for 18–22 minutes. To make sure the cupcakes are ready, insert a toothpick near the center of one. If the toothpick comes out clean, you know they are done! If any batter sticks to the toothpick, they need to bake for longer. So easy! Wow! When they cool down, you can top them with powdered sugar or a frosting.

PERFECT PAIRING: It's always a good time to pull out an old used paperback copy of Jack Kerouac's *On the Road* to peruse as you devour this chocolatey goodness. Stella recommends having a full gas tank in your car before beginning—just in case the impulse hits to embark on a road trip.

Lover's Cake

Recipe for one 8 x 8 square cake
(perfect for two to share over the weekend!)

1 1/2 cups unbleached organic flour
1/2 cup coconut oil
3/4 cup organic raw sugar
1 cup almond or coconut milk
1/2 teaspoon baking soda
1 teaspoon organic vanilla extract
1 1/2 teaspoons baking powder
1 teaspoon rum
1 teaspoon salt
1 teaspoon apple cider vinegar
1/4 cup shredded organic coconut

Preheat oven to 350 degrees. Add milk and apple cider vinegar together in a small bowl. Set aside. In a large bowl, mix all the dry ingredients together except for the shredded organic coconut. Return to the small bowl you set aside. Add the oil, rum, and vanilla to the milk mixture. Once combined well, pour the wet ingredients into the dry ingredients and mix well. The final step is to add the shredded organic coconut. Pour the batter evenly into your baking pan that has a nonstick surface, or one you prepared with cooking spray. Bake for approximately 30 minutes. To make sure the cake is ready, insert a toothpick near the center of one. If the toothpick comes out clean, you know the cake is done! If any batter sticks to the toothpick, it needs to bake for longer. When the cake cools down, drizzle with a warm rum butter glaze.

Butter Rum Glaze

In a saucepan, stir together 1/4 cup vegan butter, 2 tablespoons water, 1/2 cup organic raw sugar, and a dash of salt over medium heat. Keep stirring until the mixture boils and then stir continuously for 5 minutes. (Do not leave the mixture unattended since it might boil over.) Remove the pan from the stove. Carefully mix in 2 tablespoons to 1/4 cup rum, depending on your desired strength of rum flavor. The rum will cause the mixture to bubble as you add it, so use caution when adding. Drizzle the glaze over your cake. Enjoy!

PERFECT PAIRING: Oh! Read or sing the ancient poems and fragments of the Greek poet Sappho while digging into your lover's cake. This lush cake is best enjoyed outside under the moonlight or in bed.

A Note from the Author:
Writing a Community Novel

About a decade ago, after several years of baking experiments and receiving good feedback from people, I went through the process of getting a home bakery permit through the county where I live. I called my home bakery the Wild Librarian Bakery. The tagline was "vegan baked goods inspired by great books." I carried the permit for two years. During this time, I baked for a restaurant in downtown Santa Ana, California (around the area where Stella's bakery is located), for Food Not Bombs, at art and literary festivals here and there, and sometimes for the Catholic Worker in my community. It wasn't a serious business endeavor, but I had a lot of fun. Things creatively evolved from there.

My experiences with the Wild Librarian Bakery permit transformed into a dream of owning my own place called the Wild Librarian Bakery and Bookstore. I imagined it as a great community gathering spot with awesome baked goods, inspiring books, delicious coffee, and diverse events such as poetry readings, live music, and art workshops.

In 2016, I created the *Wild Librarian Bakery and Bookstore* zine (a zine is a self-published booklet or pamphlet like *Helen's Magical Questions* in the novel). This has been one of my most popular zines, in which I detail my dream.

In 2019, realizing having an actual place was beyond my means anytime soon, I thought of bringing my dream into the world in another way. As an artist and writer, it is through words and images that my imagination can play, and dreams may come true in other creative ways. I started writing this novel, discovering that I could bring my imaginary place into the real world and the lives of readers. During the first draft, I worked with a wonderful novelist, short story writer, and writing coach, Scott O'Connor, whom I found through Writing Workshops Los Angeles. Scott helped me develop some of my characters and scenes. Only about thirty percent of that first draft remained, but this includes a good amount of the writing I did while working with Scott, including the development of the Mary Chin character. Thank you, Scott!

After putting my first draft aside to work on other projects, I got the idea to create a children's picture book about the Wild Librarian Bakery and Bookstore dream. A book I illustrated and authored to bring the magical universe of the Wild Librarian to children was recently published by Litwin Books. When my picture book went into production, I pulled out my first draft of this novel with fresh eyes and got back to work on more drafts and revisions.

As you read the novel, you may have noticed that there is a diversity of characters. It was always my goal to write a community novel. There are young and old people. There are single, married, divorced, and widowed characters. Some characters have children; others don't. Andy and Alex, along with Barbara and Sheila, are same-sex couples. There are characters of different racial backgrounds. We also see differently abled individuals, such as Eleanor McDaniels with her walking stick and Helen Sosa with her cane. We see that romance, passion, and sex are not just the domain of the young. Some people are reserved, some are clearly extroverts (Rita Johansen!), some have deep sorrow, and others are full of joy. Some work through tragedy and overcome. The important thing for me in imagining the universe of the Wild Librarian is that everyone is loved and accepted.

Several years ago, I participated at one of the annual Howard Zinn Book Fairs in San Francisco. The hopeful theme, rooted in human rights and social justice, was "The World We Want." When I imagine this world, it is a place where all people are valued and welcomed. In this world, everyone will have somewhere to go that provides them a sense of belonging. I've never forgotten that theme of "The World We Want," and I try to create this world in my writing and art and in how I interact with and treat people as a librarian and professor. The Wild Librarian is an example of this world. This is what makes this work a community novel, and I hope you experienced it in this way.

I wish to thank my extraordinarily wonderful editor Bryony Leah (www.bryonyleah.com) for providing a thorough and incredibly detailed critique of the second draft of my manuscript and further critiques and assistance as I worked on revisions. Bryony was instrumental in helping me make this novel-in-stories better. Her engagement with the characters gave me the momentum I needed to finish what felt like a mammoth task. I'm also thankful for Mary Camarillo and Safia Gosla who read an earlier draft of the manuscript, provided helpful feedback, and encouraged me to move forward. Thank you all for believing in me and the world of the Wild Librarian!

Will the Wild Librarian Bakery and Bookstore ever exist in the real world as a place where you can come and hang out? I don't know, but I certainly don't give up on dreams. Maybe one day I will see you there and we can enjoy a cup of coffee together.

Book Club Discussion Questions

1. Do you currently have a community gathering place like the Wild Librarian in your life? If so, what do you like about it? Have there been places like the Wild Librarian in your past?
2. How important are places like the Wild Librarian in creating a sense of community and culture of belonging?
3. In the beginning of the novel-in-stories, we discover Stella left her career as a community college librarian to follow her dream and open the Wild Librarian. Is there a big dream in your life that you are hesitant to follow?
4. Many novels and movies end with a wedding involving the main character. Although Rita Johansen's story ends with her marrying John King, the novel-in-stories concludes with Stella at her own home with Chris. Although she is in a relationship, she remains unmarried. What do you think of the author's decision to conclude the final story this way?
5. Can someone be "blissfully single," as Stella describes herself? Do you know anyone you would describe this way?
6. Have you experienced a transformation in your life like Mary Chin? What happened that caused your transformation?
7. By the end of the novel-in-stories, we see Robert Gonzales able to forgive Maria for abandoning him although he suffered greatly from her actions. Have you experienced the power of forgiveness in your life? Would you be able to forgive Maria?
8. What does Tom Donald's story tell us about the healing power of art and creativity?
9. Chris Sosa awakens a desire in Stella that she was unaware she had, causing her to pursue a romance and do things out-of-character. Have you had an experience in your life, such as meeting someone, that unexpectedly changed your outlook overnight?
10. If the Wild Librarian was a real place near your home, would you be a customer?

About the Author

Stacy Russo is a California writer, poet, and artist who is committed to creating books and art for a more peaceful world. She serves as librarian and associate professor at Santa Ana College. Stacy is the author of several nonfiction books and two poetry chapbooks. She is the author and illustrator of the children's picture books *Poetry Hounds*, inspired by her dogs Joni and Walter, and *Wild Librarian Bakery and Bookstore*, which is set in the same universe as her novel-in-stories. Stacy's books have been adapted for university classes and featured on National Public Radio, Pacifica Radio, the Canadian Broadcasting System, Sirius XM Radio, *KCET Artbound*, *LA Weekly*, and various other media channels. She holds English degrees from the University of California, Berkeley and Chapman University, and a degree in library and information science from San Jose State University. She is the former chair of the Association of College and Research Libraries – Women and Gender Studies Section. After a long career as a writer working with traditional publishers, she returned to her DIY punk rock roots and created Wild Librarian Press to publish *Stella Peabody's Wild Librarian Bakery and Bookstore*, her debut novel. She is currently pursuing a PhD in transformative studies through California Institute of Integral Studies. Stacy always takes her coffee black and begins each day with a walk around her neighborhood.

www.stacy-russo.com

www.ingramcontent.com/pod-product-compliance
Lightning Source LLC
Chambersburg PA
CBHW061207210726
48294CB00006B/1779